"Now, I see you two v

"Here I was picturing
the middle of nowhe
luxurious villa above
ever seen."

Kings. Her word choice smothered Nic's amusement.
Had she used the word deliberately? Had his friend
given up all Nic's secrets?

"How can you afford a place like this? You guys were
always looking for investors for your business. It
seems to me that anyone who had enough money to
own this villa could have financed the entire project."

A little of his tension fell away, but only a little. She
didn't know the truth yet. But when she did...

Tell her. Tell her who you are.

Wise words. Pity he couldn't bring himself to follow
his own advice. He'd been hiding his true identity
from her for too long. She'd be devastated when she
learned how much he'd lied about. Yet it was only
a matter of a week before the media found out he
was wife-hunting and he went from obscure scientist
to international news item. She would know soon
enough. And hopefully when that happened she
would appreciate that they'd kept their relationship
quiet.

Because if he was to be king, she couldn't be his wife.

* * *

A Royal Baby Surprise
is part of the Sherdana Royals trilogy by Cat Schield!

Dear Reader,

Some of my books start with: What if...? The idea for this book came to me in Kioni, during a sailing trip around the Greek Ionian Islands. The town is small and charming with whitewashed houses that cling to the hillside surrounding a horseshoe-shaped harbor. The colors are vivid. The food is fantastic, and you can't beat the views along the switchback road that climbs up and up.

If you are interested in seeing some of the photos from my Kioni trip, visit me at catschield.net or find me at pinterest.com/catschieldbooks.

Happy reading!

Cat

A ROYAL BABY SURPRISE

CAT SCHIELD

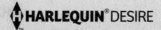

H HARLEQUIN® DESIRE

Recycling programs
for this product may
not exist in your area.

ISBN-13: 978-0-373-73406-1

A Royal Baby Surprise

This edition published by arrangement with Harlequin Books S.A.

For questions and comments about the quality of this book, please contact us at CustomerService@Harlequin.com.

Printed in U.S.A.

www.Harlequin.com

Cat Schield has been reading and writing romance since high school. Although she graduated from college with a BA in business, her idea of a perfect career was writing books for Harlequin. And now, after winning the Romance Writers of America 2010 Golden Heart® Award for series contemporary romance, that dream has come true. Cat lives in Minnesota with her daughter, Emily, and their Burmese cat. When she's not writing sexy, romantic stories for Harlequin Desire, she can be found sailing with friends on the St. Croix River, or in more exotic locales, like the Caribbean and Europe. She loves to hear from readers. Find her at catschield.net. Follow her on Twitter: @catschield.

To the 2008 Ionian Islands Crew:
Erik, Sonia, Charie, Renee, Jean and Val

One

Above the sound of the breeze blowing through the cedar trees that dotted the island hillside, Nic Alessandro heard the scuff of a footstep on flagstone and knew he wasn't alone on the terrace.

"So this is where you've been hiding." Brooke Davis's voice was like his favorite vodka: smoky and smooth, with a sexy, implied bite. And she went to his head just as swiftly.

Already suffering from a well-deserved hangover, Nic was further jolted by her unexpected arrival on this out-of-the-way Greek island. But he couldn't let himself be glad to see her. The future he'd once planned to have with her was impossible. His older brother, Gabriel, had married a woman incapable of having children, meaning he would have no son to inherit the throne of Sherdana, the European nation their family had ruled for hundreds of years. Now, as next in line to the throne, it was up to Nic to find a wife that the laws of his country would accept as the future mother of the royal line. As an American, Brooke didn't fit the bill.

"Is this the rustic cabin on the side of a mountain you told me about?" she asked. "The one you said I'd hate because it had no running water and no indoor toilets?"

Nic detected the strain she tried to hide beneath her teasing tone. What was she doing here? Had her brother Glen sent her to talk Nic into returning to California? He couldn't believe she'd come on her own after the way he'd broken things off.

"Here I was picturing you suffering in some hovel in the middle of nowhere. Instead, I find you living in a luxurious villa above the most gorgeous harbor I've ever seen."

Her voice came from the side of the terrace that led down to the beach, so she must have arrived by boat. Walking up the hundred and fifty steps hadn't winded her a bit. She loved to work out. It was what kept her lithe body in perfect shape.

What had he been thinking when he'd finally surrendered to the powerful attraction he'd hidden from her for the past five years? He shouldn't have been so quick to assume that his royal duty to Sherdana ended the minute Gabriel had gotten engaged to Lady Olivia Darcy.

"You're probably wondering how I found you."

Nic opened his eyes and watched Brooke saunter across the terrace. She wore a white, high-waisted cotton blouse and faded denim shorts with a ragged hem. The gray scarf wound around her neck was one of her favorites.

Everything she passed she touched: the back of the lounge chair, the concrete wall that bordered the terrace, the terra-cotta pots and the herbs and flowers they held. As her fingertips drifted along the fuchsia petals of a bougainvillea, Nic envied the flower she caressed.

At this hour of the morning, the sun was behind the villa, warming the front garden. On winter days he would have taken coffee to the side patio and made the most of the sunshine. In late July, he preferred the back terrace where he could enjoy the view of the town of Kioni across the harbor. The wind off the Ionian Sea kept the humidity at bay, making this a pleasant spot to linger most of the morning.

"I'm guessing Glen sent you."

She looked pained by his assumption. "No, it was my idea to come."

A double blow. She hadn't accepted the end of their relationship, and Glen didn't want him back working on the rocket after the explosion that had killed a member of their team. An explosion caused when the fuel system Nic had been working on malfunctioned. When the *Griffin* had blown up, his dream of privatizing space travel had gone up in smoke with it. He'd retreated from California in defeat, only to discover that he was now facing royal obligations back in Sherdana.

"You brought him here two years ago for a boys' weekend after a successful test firing. He came back with horror stories of long hikes in the mountains and an abundance of wildlife. I realize now those hikes involved stairs leading down to a private beach and the wildlife was in the bars in town. Shame on you two. I actually felt sorry for him."

Nic rubbed his hand across the stubble around his mouth, hiding a brief smile. They'd certainly had her going.

"Now I see you two were living like kings."

Kings. Her word choice smothered Nic's amusement. Had she used the word deliberately? Had Glen given up all Nic's secrets?

"How can you afford a place like this? You guys were always looking for investors. It seems to me that anyone who had enough money to own this villa could have financed the entire project."

A little of his tension fell away, but only a little. She didn't know the truth yet. And when she did find out...

Tell her. Tell her who you are.

Wise words. Pity he couldn't bring himself to follow his own advice. He'd been hiding his true identity from her for too long. She'd be devastated when she learned how much he'd lied about. Yet, it was only a matter of a week before the media found out he was wife-hunting and he went from obscure scientist to international news item. She would know soon enough. And hopefully when that happened she would appreciate that they'd kept their brief relationship quiet.

She believed herself in love with a man who didn't exist. A man of duty, honor and integrity. They were principles that he'd been raised to embrace, but they'd been sadly lacking the moment he'd pulled Brooke into his arms and kissed her that first time.

"My brothers and I own it," he said, wishing so many things could be different.

Brooke's very stillness suggested the calm before the storm. "I see."

That was it? No explosion? No ranting? "What do you see?"

"That we have a lot to talk about."

He didn't want to talk. He wanted to pull her into his arms and make love to her until they were both too exhausted to speak. "I've already said everything I intend to." He shouldn't have phrased that like a challenge. She was as tenacious as a terrier when she got her teeth into something.

"Don't give me that. You owe me some answers."

"Fine." He owed her more than that. "What do you want to know?"

"You have brothers?"

"Two. We're triplets."

"You never talked about your family. Why is that?"

"There's not much to say."

"Here's where we disagree."

She stepped closer. Vanilla and honey enveloped him, overpowering the scent of cypress and the odor of brine carried on the light morning breeze. With her finger she eased his dark sunglasses down his nose and captured his gaze. Her delicate brows pulled together in a frown.

He braced himself against the pitch and roll of emotions as her green-gray eyes scoured his face. He should tell her to go away, but he was so damned glad to see her that the words wouldn't come. Instead, he growled like a cranky dog that wasn't sure whether to bite or beg to be petted.

"You look like hell."

"I'm fine." Disgusted by his suddenly hoarse voice, he knocked her hand aside and slid his sunglasses back into place.

She, on the other hand, looked gorgeous. Rambunctious red hair, streaked with dark honey, framed her oval face and cascaded over her shoulders. Her pale, unblemished skin, arresting dimples and gently curving cheekbones made for the sort of loveliness any man could lose his head over. A wayward curl tickled his skin as she leaned over him. Shifting his gaze, he took the strand between two fingers and toyed with it.

"What have you been doing all alone in your fancy villa?" she asked.

"If you must know, I'm working."

"On your tan maybe." She sniffed him and wrinkled her slender nose. "Or a hangover. Your eyes are bloodshot."

"I've been working late."

"Riiight." She drew the word out doubtfully. "I'll make some coffee. It looks like you could use some."

Safe behind his dark glasses, he watched her go, captivated by the gentle sway of her denim-clad rear and her long legs. Satin smooth skin stretched over lean muscles, honed by yoga and running. His pulse purred as he recalled those strong, shapely legs wrapped around his hips.

Despite the cool morning air, his body heated. An hour ago, he'd opened his eyes, feeling as he had most of the past few mornings: queasy, depressed and distraught over the accident that had occurred during a test firing of their prototype rocket ship.

Brooke's arrival on this sleepy, Greek island was like being awakened from a drugged sleep by an air horn.

"Someone must be taking care of you," she said a short time later, bringing the smell of bitter black coffee with her when she returned. "The coffeepot was filled with grounds and water. All I had to do was turn it on."

Nic's nostrils flared eagerly as he inhaled the robust aroma. The scent alone was enough to bring him back to life.

She sat down on the lounge beside his and cradled her mug between both hands. She took a tentative sip and made a face. "Ugh. I forgot how strong you like it."

He grunted and willed the liquid to cool a little more so he could drain his cup and start on a second. It crossed his mind that coping with Brooke while a strong jolt of stimulant rushed through his veins was foolhardy at best. She riled him up admirably all by herself, making the mix of caffeine and being alone with her a lethal combination.

"So, am I interrupting a romantic weekend?"

Luckily he hadn't taken another sip, or the stuff might have come straight out his nose. His fingers clenched around the mug. When they began to cramp, he ground his teeth and relaxed his grip.

"Probably not," she continued when he didn't answer. "Or you'd be working harder to get rid of me."

Damn her for showing up while his guard was down. Temptation rode him like a demon every time she was near.

But he couldn't have her. She mustn't know how much he wanted her. He'd barely summoned the strength to break things off a month ago. But now that he was alone with her on this island, her big misty-green eyes watching his every mood, would his willpower hold out?

Silence stretched between them. He heard the creak of wood as she settled back on the lounge. He set the empty cup on his chest and closed his eyes once more. Having her here brought him a sense of peace he had no right to feel. He wanted to reach out and lace his fingers with hers but didn't dare to.

"I can see why you and your brothers bought this place. I could sit here for days and stare at the view."

Nic snorted softly. Brooke had never been one to sit anywhere and stare at anything. She was a whirling dervish of energy and enthusiasm.

"I can't believe how blue the water is. And the town is so quaint. I can't wait to go exploring."

Exploring? Nic needed to figure out how to get her on a plane back to America as soon as possible before he gave in to temptation. Given her knack for leading with her emotions, reasoning with her wouldn't work. Threats wouldn't work, either. The best technique for dealing with Brooke was to let her have her way and that absolutely couldn't happen this time. Or ever again, for that matter.

When she broke the silence, the waver in her voice betrayed worry. "When are you coming back?"

"I'm not."

"You can't mean that." She paused, offering him the opportunity to take back what he'd said. When he didn't, her face took on a troubled expression. "You do mean that. What about *Griffin*? What about the team? You can't just give it all up."

"Someone died because of a flaw in a system I designed—"

She gripped his forearm. "Glen was the one pushing for the test. He didn't listen when you told him it wasn't ready. He's the one to blame."

"Walter died." He enunciated the words, letting her hear his grief. "It was my fault."

"So that's it? You are giving up because something went wrong? You expect me to accept that you're throwing away your life's work? To do what?"

He had no answer. What the hell was he going to do in Sherdana besides get married and produce an heir? He had no interest in helping run the country. That was Gabriel's job. And his other brother Christian had his businesses and investments to occupy him. All Nic wanted to do, all he'd ever wanted to do, was build rockets that would someday carry people into space. With that possibility extinguished, his life stretched before him, empty and filled with regret.

"There's something else going on." She tightened her grip on his arm. "Don't insult my intelligence by denying it."

Nic patted her hand. "I would never do that, Dr. Davis." A less intelligent woman wouldn't have captivated him so completely, no matter how beautiful. Brooke's combination of sex appeal and brains had delivered a fatal one-two punch. "How many doctorates do you have now, anyway?"

"Only two." She jerked her hand from beneath his, reacting to his placating tone. "And don't change the subject." Despite her annoyance, a huge yawn practically dislocated her jaw as she glared at him.

"You're tired." Showing concern for her welfare might encourage her, but he couldn't help it.

"I've been on planes since yesterday sometime. Do you know how long it takes to get here?" She closed her eyes. "About twenty hours. And I couldn't sleep on the flight over."

"Why?"

A deep breath pushed her small, pert breasts tight against her sleeveless white cotton blouse.

"Because I was worried about you, that's why."

The admission was a cop-out. It was fourth on her list of reasons why she'd flown six thousand miles to talk to him in person rather than breaking her news over the phone.

But she wasn't prepared to blurt out that she was eight weeks pregnant within the first ten minutes of arriving.

She had a lot of questions about why he'd broken off their relationship four weeks earlier. Questions she hadn't asked at first because she'd been too hurt to wonder why he'd dropped her when things between them had been so perfect. Then the fatal accident had happened with *Griffin*. Nic had left California and she'd never received closure.

"I don't need your concern," he said.

"Of course you don't." She crammed all the skepticism she could muster into her tone to keep from revealing how much his rebuff stung. "That's why you look like week-old roadkill."

Although his expression didn't change, his voice reflected amusement. "Nice image."

She surveyed his disheveled state, thought about the circles she'd seen beneath his eyes, their utter lack of vitality. The thick black stubble on his cheeks made her wonder how long it had been since he'd shaved. No matter how hard he worked, she'd never seen his golden-brown eyes so flat and lifeless. He really did look like death warmed over.

"Brooke, why did you really come here?"

Her ready excuse died on her lips. He'd believe that she'd come here to convince him to return to the project. It would be safe to argue on behalf of her brother. But where Nic was concerned, she hadn't played it safe for five years. He deserved the truth. So, she selected item number three on her list of why she'd chased after him.

"You disappeared without saying goodbye." Once she better understood what had spooked him, Brooke would confess the number one reason she'd followed him to Ithaca. "When you didn't answer any of my phone calls or respond to my emails, I decided to come find you." She gathered a fortifying breath before plunging into deep water. "I want to know the real reason why things ended between us."

Nic tunneled his fingers into his shaggy black hair, a sure sign he was disturbed. "I told you—"

"That I was too distracting." She glared at him. Nic was her polar opposite. Always so serious, he never let go like other people. He held himself apart from the fun. She'd treated his solemnity as a challenge. And after years of escalating flirtation, she'd discovered he wasn't as in control as he appeared. "You weren't getting enough work done."

She exhaled in exasperation. For five months he'd stopped working on the weekends she'd visited and spent that entire time focused on her. All that attention had been heady and addictive. Brooke hadn't anticipated that he might wake up one morning and go back to his workaholic ways. "I don't get it. We were fantastic together. You were happy."

Nic's mouth tightened into a grim line. "It was fun. But you were all in and I wasn't."

Brooke bit her lip and considered what he said for an awkward, silent minute. "You broke up with me because I told you I loved you?" At the time she hadn't worried about confessing her feelings. After all, she was pretty sure he suspected she'd been falling for him for five years. "Did you ever intend to give us a chance?"

"I thought it was better to end it rather than to let things drag out. I was wrong to let things get so involved between us."

"Why didn't you tell me this in the first place?"

"I thought it would be easier on you if you believed I'd chosen work over you."

"Instead of being truthful and admitting I wasn't the one."

This wasn't how she'd expected this conversation to go. Deep in her heart she'd believed Nic was comfortable with how fast their relationship had progressed. She'd been friends with him long enough to know he didn't squander his time away from the *Griffin* project. This led her to believe she mattered to him. How could she have been so wrong?

Conflicting evidence tugged her thoughts this way and that. Usually she considered less and acted more, but being pregnant meant her actions impacted more than just her. She needed a little time to figure out how to approach Nic about her situation.

"I guess my optimistic nature got the better of me again." She lightened her tone to hide the deep ache centered in her chest.

"Brooke—"

"Don't." She held up both hands to forestall whatever he'd planned to say. "Why don't we not talk about this anymore while you give me a tour of your palatial estate."

"It's not palatial." His thick black eyebrows drew together in a grim frown.

"It is to a girl who grew up in a three-bedroom, fifteen-hundred-square-foot house."

Nic's only reply was a grunt. He got to his feet and gestured for her to precede him. Before entering the house, Brooke kicked off her sandals. The cool limestone tile soothed her tired feet as she slipped past him. Little brush fires ignited along her bare arm where it came into contact with his hair-roughened skin.

"This is the combination living-dining room and

kitchen," he said, adopting the tour guide persona he used when escorting potential *Griffin* investors.

She took in the enormous abstract paintings of red, yellow, blue and green that occupied the wall behind the white slip-covered couches. To her left, in the L-shaped kitchen, there was a large glass table with eight black chairs, offering a contrast among the white cabinets and stainless appliances. The space had an informal feel that invited relaxation.

"The white furniture and walls are a little stark for my taste," she said. "But it works with the paintings. They're wonderful. Who did them?"

"My sister."

He had a sister, too? "I'd like to meet her." Even as Brooke spoke the words, she knew that would never happen. Nic had made it perfectly clear he didn't want her in his life. She had a decision to make in the next day or so. It was why she'd come here. She needed his help to determine how the rest of her life would play out. "Did Glen know about your family?"

"Yes."

That hurt. The two men had always been as tight as brothers, but she never expected that Glen would keep secrets from her.

"Tell me about your brothers." She didn't know what to make of all these revelations.

"We're triplets. I'm the middle one."

"Two brothers and a sister," she murmured.

Who was Nic Alessandro? At the moment he looked nothing like the overworked rocket scientist she'd known for years. Although a bit wrinkled and worse for wear, his khaki shorts and white short-sleeved shirt had turned him into an ad for Armani's summer collection. In fact, his expensive sunglasses and elegant clothes transformed him from an absentminded scientist into your basic, run-of-the-mill European playboy. The makeover shifted him further out of reach.

"Is there anyone else I should know about?" Despite her best efforts to keep her tone neutral, her voice had an edge. "Like a wife?"

"No wife."

Brooke almost smiled at his dark tone. Once upon a time she'd taken great delight in teasing him, and it should have been easy to fall back into that kind of interaction. Unfortunately, the first time he'd kissed her, she'd crossed into a deeply serious place where his rejection had the power to bruise and batter her heart.

"Who takes care of all this when you're not here?" Keeping the conversation casual was the only way to keep sadness from overwhelming her.

"We have a caretaker who lives in town. She comes in once a week to clean when we're not in residence, more often when we are. She also cooks for us, and her husband maintains the gardens and the boat, and fixes whatever needs repairing in the house."

Brooke looked over her shoulder at the outdoor terrace with its informal wood dining table and canvas chairs. A set of three steps led down to another terrace with more lounge chairs. Potted herbs lined the three-foot-high walls, softening all the concrete.

"What's upstairs?"

Nic stood in the middle of the living room, his arms crossed, a large, immovable object. "Bedrooms."

"One I can use?" she asked in a small voice.

A muscle twitched in his jaw. "There are a number of delightful hotels in town."

"You'd turn me out?" Something flared in his eyes that brought her hope back to life. Maybe she hadn't yet heard the complete explanation for why he'd broken off their relationship. She faked a sniffle. "You can't really be so mean as to send me in search of a hotel when you have so much room here."

Nic growled. "I'll show you where you can shower and grab some sleep before you head home."

Although it stung that he was so eager to get rid of her, she'd departed California suspecting he wouldn't welcome her intrusion.

"Then, I can stay?"

"For the moment."

Mutely, she followed him back out through the open French doors and onto the terrace. He made a beeline toward the duffel bag she'd dropped beside the stairs that lead up from the beach.

"I can't get over how beautiful it is here."

"Most people are probably more familiar with the islands in the Aegean," he said, picking up her bag. "Mykonos, Santorini, Rhodes."

"I imagine there's a lot more tourists there."

"Quite a few. Kioni attracts a number of sailors during the summer as well as some people wanting to hike and enjoy a quieter island experience, but we're not overrun. Come on, the guesthouse is over there." He led the way along the terrace to a separate building.

"You should take me sightseeing."

"No. You are going to rest and then we're going to find you a flight home."

Brooke rolled her eyes at Nic's words and decided to take the fact that he kept trying to be rid of her as a challenge. "My return ticket is for a flight a week from now."

"Don't you have a lot to do to prepare for your students at Berkeley?"

"I don't have the job yet." Though Brooke held a position at UC Santa Cruz, teaching Italian studies at Berkeley had been a dream of hers since her sophomore year in college. And then she and Nic had begun a relationship. Soon the distance from San Francisco to the Mojave Desert had become an impediment to what she wanted: a life with Nic.

He shot her a sharp look.

She shrugged. "The interview got postponed again."

"To when?"

"Not for a few weeks yet."

In truth she wasn't sure when it was. There'd been some scheduling conflicts with the head of the department. He'd already canceled two meetings with her in the past month. Not knowing how many people were up for the position she wanted gnawed at her confidence. Few shared her research credentials, but a great many had more experience in the classroom than she did.

And before Nic had abruptly dumped her, she'd begun thinking she wanted to be closer to where he lived and worked. Seeing him only on the weekends wasn't enough. So she'd interviewed for a position at UCLA and been offered a teaching job starting in the fall. The weekend Nic had come up to San Francisco to break up with her, she'd been preparing for a very different conversation. One where she told him she was moving to LA. Only he'd beaten her to the punch and she'd decided to put the Berkeley job back on the table.

"Are you sure?" Nic questioned. "It's July. I can't believe they want to put off their decision too much longer."

She frowned at him, butterflies hatching in her stomach as she realized the risk she'd taken by flying here when she should be waiting by the phone in California. "Yes, I'm sure."

"Because I couldn't live with myself if you lost your dream job because you stayed here imagining I'm going to change my mind about us."

Had she been wrong about his initial reaction to her arrival? Had she so badly wanted him to be glad to see her that she'd imagined the delight in his gaze? It wouldn't be the first time she'd jumped to the wrong conclusion where a man's behavior was concerned. And Nic was a master at keeping his thoughts and emotions hidden.

"Don't worry about my dream job," she countered. "It will still be there when I get back."

She hoped.

When they arrived at the small guesthouse, Nic pushed open the door and set her luggage inside. "There's a private bathroom and a great view of Kioni. You should be comfortable here." Neither his impassive expression nor his neutral tone gave anything away. "Relax. Sleep. I'm sure you're exhausted from your travels. Breakfast will be waiting when you're ready."

"I'm not really hungry." Between morning sickness and anxiety, her appetite had fled. "And no matter how tired I am, you know I can't sleep when the sun is up. Why don't we go into town and you can show me around."

"You should rest."

His tone warned her not to argue. The wall he'd erected between them upset her. She wanted to tear it down with kisses and tears and impassioned pleas for him to change his mind about breaking up. But a big emotional scene would only cause him to retreat. She needed to appeal to that big logical brain of his.

"I've come a long way to find you. And talk."

"Later." He scowled at her to forestall any further discussion.

The determined set of his mouth told her she would get nowhere until he was ready to listen. She nodded, reluctant to provoke Nic into further impatience. She wanted him in a calm, agreeable state of mind when she imparted her dramatic news.

Left alone, Brooke took a quick shower in the white, marble bathroom and dressed in a tribal-print maxi dress of cool cotton. There was enough of a breeze blowing in through the open windows to dry her hair, but she didn't want to give Nic too much time to plan his strategy for getting her to leave. She decided to braid the damp strands rather than leave them loose. The last time they'd made love a little over a month ago, he'd shown a great appreciation for the disarray of her long, curly tresses, but now it seemed better to approach him logically and for that she needed to be restrained, not flirty.

Unfortunately, the mirror over the dresser reflected a woman in love, with wide eyes and a slightly unfocused gaze. Her mouth had a rosy fullness and her cheeks were pink. She doubted that this would go over well with Nic.

And after what he'd told her about his reasons for breaking up, Brooke was certain her pregnancy news would be unwelcome, too.

She hadn't given much thought to what came after she told Nic the news. Maybe she was afraid to face more rejection. What if he wanted nothing further to do with her? He'd said he wasn't returning to California. Would the news that he was going to be a father change his plans?

Brooke slid her feet into sandals, but paused before leaving the room. Talking with Nic about her Berkeley interview reminded her she hadn't checked her messages since leaving San Francisco. She dug her cell phone out of the side pocket of her duffel bag and tried to turn it on, but the battery had died. Time ticked away as she dug out her charger and searched for the adapter she'd borrowed. Then there were the minutes it took for the phone to charge enough to come back to life. By the time the display lit up and showed she'd missed a dozen calls, Brooke crackled with impatience.

Her heart sank as she listened to the messages. Her Berkeley interview had been rescheduled for 10:00 a.m. three days from now. This considerably shortened the amount of time Brooke had to tell Nic she was pregnant and figure out what form her future relationship with him would take. A quick check of flight schedules revealed that it would be daunting, but doable.

Brooke tossed the phone onto the middle of the bed and took several deep breaths until the tightness in her throat eased. After a few more deep breaths, the urge to throw herself onto the mattress and scream into a pillow subsided, too. Everything would work out just fine. Somehow it always did.

Applying a bright smile to her face, she strolled along the terrace. But as she stepped into the living room of the main house, the absolute quiet told her something was awry. A quick check confirmed her suspicions, but what clinched it was the car missing from the driveway.

Nic had vanished.

Two

Nic had switched from Greek coffee to beer by the time Brooke showed up in Kioni, the village rising from the harbor to cling to the side of Ithaca's rocky hills. From the shade beneath the taverna's white awning, he squinted against the bright sunlight sparkling off the cerulean water and watched his thirty-four-foot cruiser pull alongside the quay. Three Greek men, each wearing broad smiles, converged to issue instructions and help Brooke settle the boat. Although the distance prevented Nic from hearing their conversation, from Brooke's animated gestures and the men's cheerful faces, he guessed she was chattering away and doing what she did best: charming men.

"You're not drinking them as fast today."

Nic switched his attention to the voluptuous, dark-haired, dark-eyed waitress standing at his side. Natasa had waited on him all but one of the past ten days he'd been on the island. She picked up his half-full bottle, which he'd been nursing for the past hour.

"I'm not as thirsty."

Since arriving on Ithaca, Nic had been keeping himself anesthetized with boredom and beer. The combination was barely enough to keep his demons at bay. Before Brooke's arrival he'd given himself a week or so before he had to make peace with his failures and accept his fate. Now it was all coming to a head faster than he could handle.

Natasa gave him a smoky look and set her hand on her hip. "Perhaps you need some company."

Nic hadn't seen her flirt with any of the other men that came to the taverna, only him. He figured she knew who he was and suspected that had prompted her offer. Acid churned in his gut. Being treated like a personality rather than a person was something he hadn't had to endure in America. He hadn't had to be on his guard and question everyone's motives.

"I get off in two hours," she continued. "I would be happy to join you then."

Natasa had made him a similar proposition last night at closing time. Nic had been moderately drunk, but not enough to wish to share the bed with this woman, no matter how attractive she was. His carefree bachelor days had ended a month ago with Gabriel's marriage. Soon every woman he glanced at twice would become fodder for news stories.

It was worse for him being in Europe than living in America. In California he was an anonymous scientist trying to build a rocket ship. On this side of the Atlantic, he was known as Prince Nicolas, second in line to the throne of Sherdana. Avoiding reporters and paparazzi and being wary of helpful strangers had become a routine part of his life. That's why he and his brothers had chosen Ithaca as a retreat. Homer had described the island as "good for goats" but it gave the Alessandro brothers an escape from their hectic world.

Not that Nic was a fool. He knew his "anonymity" on this sleepy island was tenuous at best. But he and his brothers maintained a low profile, and the locals generously pretended the Sherdanian royals were like any other part-time inhabitants.

"I'm afraid I'm already due for some company," Nic said, nodding toward the harbor.

When the boat was snugly tied, three tanned hands extended to help Brooke onto the quay. She seemed to hesitate before accepting the hands of the two men nearest to her and offering the third man an engaging smile.

Natasa shielded her eyes as she gazed in the same direction Nic was looking. "Isn't that your boat?" Her keen black eyes narrowed as she glanced at him for confirmation.

"Yes."

"And the girl?"

"She's staying with me for a few days." Until the words left his lips he hadn't realized he'd changed his mind about putting her on a plane home as soon as humanly possible. Keeping her around was a mistake, but he was feeling battered and raw. Her company was the balm his psyche needed. He just needed to keep her at arm's length.

Natasa sniffed and tossed her head. Then, without another word, she turned to go. Nic gave a mental shrug. He'd retreated to Ithaca to come to grips with his future, not to tumble into some local's bed. He liked his own company. In fact, most days, he preferred it. Why didn't people understand that and leave him alone?

Reality smacked Nic right between the eyes. Soon enough he'd never be left alone again. Returning to Sherdana meant not only a return to duty, but also a complete loss of privacy and peace. Long, solitary hours in his workshop would be a thing of the past. His father and brothers would ensure that his calendar was packed with meetings, speeches and public appearances. He'd been absent for ten years, five years of studying and another five working with Glen on the *Griffin* project.

Now that he was returning home for good, his family would expect him to get up to speed on a variety of political, economic and environmental issues affecting the country. He would be surrounded by advisers, besieged by demands for decisions and sought after for his opinions.

Balls and state dinners with visiting foreign dignitaries would replace basketball tournaments and pig roasts with the team of specialists that he'd assembled to help build the *Griffin* rocket ship. Then there would be the selection of his bride. Once his mother finished narrowing the field of marriage prospects—women his brother had already rejected—Nic would have to choose whom he would spend the rest of his life with. And he wouldn't be allowed to dawdle over his decision because the succession needed to be secured by the birth of a royal heir.

The burden of what lay ahead of him sat on Nic's shoulders like a sack of cement. Was it any wonder he'd kept Brooke in the dark about his true identity all these years? He would have liked to continue pretending that he was just an ordinary man instead of a royal prince in serious trouble of doing the wrong thing with the right woman. But she'd never agree to back off unless she knew his whole story.

In disgruntled admiration, Nic followed Brooke's progress as she made her way around the horseshoe-shaped harbor. Since he'd left the house, she'd changed into an earth-toned sundress and accessorized with chunky bracelets and a peace sign necklace. Her red hair lay in a braided rope across her left shoulder. The breeze that frolicked through the streets teased the strands around her face that weren't long enough to be restricted by the braid.

Gulls jeered as they swooped past her. She appeared

oblivious to their taunts, focused as she was on scanning the quay. The hem of the sundress brushed her calves as she walked. The thin spaghetti straps were too narrow to hide a bra so he knew she was at least partially bare beneath the dress. Speculating on just how bare renewed the pounding in his head despite the aspirin he'd taken earlier.

She neared the taverna. Nic wasn't sure she'd spotted him yet. Eight restaurants edged the water. This particular taverna was Nic's favorite. He'd sampled enough of the menu in the years since they'd bought the villa to be able to make recommendations. The waitstaff always kept the cold beer coming while he took in the view of the vivid blue harbor, a welcome change from the beige and russet California desert where he'd spent the past several years.

For entertainment he liked to watch the comings and goings of the sailboats chartered by vacationers. The captains often wrestled with the difficulties presented by Mediterranean mooring, the docking technique where the anchor was dropped forty feet into the harbor and then the boat was backed up against the cement quay. Only an hour ago he'd been witness to what could go wrong when you had twenty boats snugged in side by side. One departing boat had lifted its anchor, catching its neighbor's as it went, only to at last drop that anchor across the lines belonging to the boat on the other side, hopelessly tangling the two boats. To Nic's amusement, much shouting and gesturing had accompanied the maneuver.

His earlier question about whether Brooke had spotted him was answered as she wove through the tables, aiming straight for him.

"Where did you get the keys to the boat?" he quizzed as she plopped a big canvas purse on the table and sat down with a whoosh of breath.

"Elena showed up shortly after you left. She fed me breakfast and told me where to find them. She's very nice.

And had flattering things to say about you. I think you're her favorite triplet."

Nic wondered what else Elena had said. Had the housekeeper divulged the rest of his secret?

"I doubt that very much. She's always been partial to Christian. He's the youngest. And the one all the ladies love."

"Why is that?"

"He's not as serious as Gabriel or me."

"What does he do?"

"He buys companies and takes them apart so he can sell off the pieces."

"And Gabriel?"

"He runs the family business." Not the truth, but not exactly a lie.

"And your sister paints."

"Ariana."

"And you build rocket ships. Sounds like you're all successful."

Not all of them. With the failure of his life's work, he certainly wasn't feeling particularly successful at the moment.

"I hope you don't mind, but I used your computer to print out some forms I needed to sign."

Even while on vacation the Alessandro triplets were often working on a project or a deal and having a state-of-the-art computer as well as a combination printer and scanner often came in handy.

"You figured out how to turn it on?"

As brilliant as she was when it came to learning languages or analyzing Italian literature, Brooke was technically challenged. She'd handwritten most of her first thesis until Nic had taken her to buy a laptop. He'd then lost an entire weekend to teaching her the ins and outs of the word-processing software as well as an app that enabled her to organize her research for easy reference.

"Ha-ha. I'm not as inept as you think I am."

"That's not saying much."

She pulled a face at him. "You had about forty unopened emails from the team. Why haven't you answered any of their questions?"

Nic shifted his gaze to the harbor and watched an inbound sailboat. "As I explained to you earlier, I'm done."

"How can you walk away from your team and all the hard work they've put in on the project?"

Why didn't she understand? Even if it wasn't his duty to return to Sherdana, Nic couldn't let go of the fact that his faulty design had destroyed the rocket and resulted in a man's death. Besides, Glen was the heart of the project. He would carry on in Nic's absence.

"Glen will find a new engineer," Nic said. "Work will continue."

The rocket's destruction had hastened the inevitable. Nic had known he couldn't stay in California forever. It was only a matter of time before responsibility to his country would have forced him to return home.

"But you were the brains behind the new fuel delivery system."

And his life's work had resulted in a complete disaster. "They have my notes."

"But—"

"Leave it alone." He kept his voice low, but the sharp snap of the words silenced her. An uneasy tension descended between them. "Are you hungry? If you like eggplant, the moussaka is very good."

She pressed her lips together, but Nic could see she wanted to argue with him further. Instead, she asked, "So, what are you going to do?"

"My family is going through a hard time right now. I'm going home."

"For how long?"

"For good."

"Wow."

The shaky breath she released was a punch to his gut. A week ago he'd left California as soon as the initial investigation of the accident concluded. He hadn't spoken to her before getting on a plane. His emotions were too raw. And he'd had no idea how to say goodbye.

"I wish I could make you understand, but I can't."

"You're afraid."

Nic eyed Brooke. Her perceptiveness where he was concerned had always made him wary of letting her get too close. Maybe telling her the truth would be a mistake. Giving her access to his life would increase his connection to her, and keeping his distance would become that much harder.

"Of hurting more people, yes."

She would assume he meant another scientist like Walter Parry, the man who'd died. But Nic was thinking about his family and her brother. And most of all her. When Gabriel's engagement had been announced, Nic had felt a loosening of the ties that bound him to Sherdana. Gabriel and Olivia would get married and go on to produce the future monarchs of Sherdana, raising them with Gabriel's twin two-year-old daughters, Bethany and Karina, who'd come to live with Gabriel after their fashion model mother had died a month earlier. They were illegitimate and the only children Gabriel would ever have.

Lady Olivia's infertility—and Gabriel's decision to make her his wife—meant Nic and Christian were no longer free to marry whomever they wished. Or, in Christian's case, to continue enjoying his playboy lifestyle and never marry at all.

Nic cursed the circumstances that had turned his life upside down and sucked him back into a world that couldn't include Brooke. If he'd been a simple scientist, he wouldn't have to resist the invitation in her eyes. Nic shoved away the traitorous thought. It was pointless to dwell on what could never be.

"I can't believe you're really going to give it all up," she said. "You and my brother were excited about the future. The pair of you would get so caught up in a new discovery you wouldn't have noticed if a tornado swept the lab away. You love being a scientist."

"I do, but…" In the three weeks since the rocket had blown up, he'd lost confidence in his abilities. Yet his passion continued to burn. The opposing forces were slowly tearing him apart.

"What are you going to do when you go home?"

"My brothers are interested in luring technology-based companies into the country. They want me to be their technical consultant."

He tried to inject some enthusiasm into his voice and failed. While he agreed with Gabriel that Sherdana's economy would benefit from an influx of such businesses, he wasn't excited about his role in the process. His whole life he'd been actively engaged in creating technologies that would shape the future. The idea of promoting someone else's vision depressed him.

"Sooo," she dragged the word out, "you're never coming back to California?"

"No."

"If this is about the rocket…"

"It's not."

"I don't understand what's going on with you." She looked more than puzzled. She looked worried. "It's not like you to give up."

Nic knew she deserved a full explanation, but once she

found out he'd been keeping a huge secret from her all these years she was going to be furious. "There's a little something about me you don't know."

"Oh, I think there's more than a little something."

He ignored her sarcasm. "It's complicated."

"It's okay. As you pointed out earlier, I have two doctorates. I can understand complicated."

"Very well. I'm not an ordinary scientist." He lowered his voice, wishing he'd had this conversation with her at the villa. "I'm Prince Nicolas Alessandro, second in line to the throne of Sherdana."

"A prince? Like a real prince?" Her misty-green eyes blurred and she shook her head as if to rid her brain of his admission. "I don't get it. You sound as American as I do."

"I went to college in Boston. In order to fit in, I eliminated my accent." Nic leaned forward, glad that there was a table between them. He longed to pull her into his arms and kiss away her unhappiness. That was something he could never again do. "My country is Sherdana. It's a small kingdom tucked between France and Italy."

"How small?"

"A little less than two thousand square kilometers with a population of just over four hundred thousand. We're mostly known for our—"

"Wines." She slapped her palm on the table. His beer rattled against the hard surface. "Now I remember why the name is so familiar. Glen had bottles of Sherdanian wine at one of his recent parties."

Nic remembered that evening without pleasure. "It was his way of sending me a message. He wanted me to tell you the truth."

She stared at Nic with dawning horror. "You jerk. I've known you for five years. And you've kept this huge thing from me the whole time? What did you think I was going to do with the information? Sell you out to the press? Torment you with Disney references? Well, that I would have done, but you're a prince—you could have handled that."

Nic waited for her rant to wind down, but she was on a roll and wasn't going to be stopped until she had her say.

"I thought we were friends." Below the irritation in her voice, she sounded as if her heart was breaking. "Why didn't you tell me any of this?"

"I've concealed my identity for a lot of years. It's a hard habit to break."

"Concealed it from strangers, coworkers, acquaintances." The breath she needed to take wasn't available. "How long has my brother known? Probably since you met. You two are as close as brothers." She shut her eyes. "Imagine how I feel, Nic. You've been lying to me as long as I've known you."

"Glen said—"

"Glen?" She pinned him with a look of such fury that a lesser man would have thrown himself at her feet to grovel for forgiveness. "My brother did not tell you to lie to me."

No. Nic had decided to do that all on his own. "He told me you'd never leave it alone if you knew."

"Are you kidding me?" Her eyes widened in dismay. "You were worried that I'd come on even stronger if I knew you were a prince? Is that how low your opinion is of me?"

"No. That's not what I meant—"

"I came here looking for scientist Nic," she reminded him. "That's the man I thought I knew. Who I've—"

"Brooke, stop." Nic badly needed to cut off her declaration.

"—fallen in love with."

Pain, hot and bright, sliced into his chest. "Damn it. I never wanted that." Which was his greatest lie to date.

"Was that how you felt before or after we became intimate?"

"Both." Hoping to distract her, he said, "Do you have any idea how irresistible you are?"

"Is that supposed to make me feel better?"

"It's supposed to explain why I started a relationship with you six months ago after I'd successfully withstood the attraction between us for the last five years."

"Why did you fight it?" She frowned "What happened between us was amazing and real."

His breath exploded from his lungs in a curse. "A month ago we had this conversation. I thought you understood."

"A month ago you claimed your work was the most important thing in your life. Now I find out you never had deep feelings for me and didn't mean to mislead me about where our relationship was heading. But I've always been of the opinion that a woman should react to how a man behaves, not what he says, and you acted like a very happy man when we were together."

"I was happy. But I was wrong to give you the impression I could offer you any kind of future."

"Because you don't care about me?"

"Because I have to go home."

Her brows drew together. "You didn't think I would go with you?"

"You have a life in California. Family. Friends. A career."

"So instead of asking me what I wanted, you made the decision for me."

"Except I can't ask." His frustration was no less acute than hers. "A month ago my older brother made a decision that affects not only my life, but the future of Sherdana."

"What sort of decision?"

"He married a woman who can never have children."

Brooke stared at him in mystified silence for a long moment before saying, "That's very sad, but what does it have to do with you?"

"It's now up to me to get married and make sure the Alessandro royal blood line is continued."

"You're going to marry?" She sat back, her hands falling from the table onto her lap.

"So that I can produce an heir. I'm second in line to the throne. It's my duty."

Her expression flattened into blank shock for several seconds as she absorbed his declaration. He'd never seen her dumbfounded. Usually she had a snappy retort for everything. Her quick mind processed at speeds that constantly amazed him.

"Your younger brother can't do it?"

The grim smile he offered her conveyed every bit of his displeasure. "I'm quite certain mother intends to see that we are both married before the year is out."

"It is a truth universally acknowledged," she quoted, "that a single man in possession of a good fortune, must be in want of a wife." She stared at the taverna's logo printed in blue on the white place mat as if the answers to the universe were written there in code. "And I'm not the one you want."

"It isn't that simple." He gripped his beer in both hands to keep from reaching out and offering her comfort. "In order for my child to be eligible to ascend Sherdana's throne someday, the constitution requires that his mother has to be either a Sherdana citizen or a member of Europe's aristocracy."

"And I'm just an ordinary girl from California with two doctorates." The corners of her mouth quivered in a weak attempt at a smile. "I get it."

Three

Beneath the grapevines woven through the taverna's roof beams, the afternoon heat pressed in on Brooke. Light-headed and slightly ill, she didn't realize how much she'd set her hopes on Nic's returning to California and giving their relationship another try until he crushed her dreams with his confession. Her fingers fanned over her still-flat abdomen and the child that grew there. Not once since she'd learned she was pregnant had she considered raising this child utterly on her own. Nic had always been there for her. First as her brother's friend. Then her friend. And finally as her lover.

When she'd strayed from her topic during the writing of her second thesis he'd spent hours on the phone talking her through her research and her arguments. He'd gone with her to buy both her cars. He always shared his dessert with her when they went out to dinner even though she knew it drove him crazy that she never ordered her own. And in a dozen little ways, he stayed present in her life even though physically they lived miles apart.

For an instant she recalled the last time she and Nic had made love. She'd gazed deep into his eyes and glimpsed her future. During their time together, their lovemaking had been in turn fast, hot, slow and achingly sweet. But on their last night in particular, they'd both been swept away by urgent intensity. Yet there'd been a single look suspended between one breath and the next that held her transfixed. In that instant, an important connection had been made between them and she'd been forever changed.

But now…

A prince.

The conversion from distracted, overworked scientist to intense, sexy aristocrat had been apparent when she'd arrived this morning. At first she'd ascribed the change to his European-style clothing, but now she understood he'd been transformed in a far more elemental manner.

A month ago he'd given her a speech about how he needed to refocus on *Griffin*, and that meant he had to stop seeing her. She'd been frustrated by the setback, but figured it was only a matter of time until he figured out they were meant to be together. When he'd left California in the wake of the accident, the bond had stretched and thinned, but it had held. Awareness of Nic had hummed across that psychic filament. Although compelled to track him down and investigate if her instincts were correct, she'd decided to give him some space to process the accident before she followed him. Her pregnancy had made finding him much more urgent.

But what good was the bond between them when the reality was he was a prince who needed to find a wife so he could father children that would one day rule his country?

And what about her own child? This was no longer a simple matter of being pregnant with Nic's baby. She was carrying the illegitimate child of a prince. For a moment the taverna spun sickeningly around her. Telling Nic he was going to be a father had become that much more complicated.

Somehow she found the strength of will to summon a wry smile. "Besides, you and I both know I'm not princess material."

"You'd hate it," Nic told her in somber tones. To her relief he'd taken her self-deprecating humor at face value. "All the restrictions on how you dressed and behaved."

"Being polite to people instead of setting them straight." He was right. She'd hate it. "The endless parties to attend where I had to smile until my face hurt. I'm so not the type."

The litany leached away her optimism. With hope reaching dangerously low levels, she cursed the expansive hollowness inside her. Nothing had felt the same since she'd stepped onto this island. It wasn't just Nic's fancy clothes, expensive villa and the whole prince thing. He was different. And more unreachable than ever.

How am I supposed to live without you?

The question lodged in her throat. She concentrated on breathing evenly to keep the tears at bay.

"Are you okay?"

Her pulse spiked at his concerned frown. In moments like these he surprised her by being attuned to her mood. And keeping track of how she was feeling was no small task. Her family often teased her about being a drama girl. She enjoyed life to the fullest, reveling in each success and taking disappointments as world-ending. As she'd gotten older, she'd learned to temper her big emotions and act on impulse less frequently.

Except where Nic was concerned. Common sense told her if she'd behave more sensibly, Nic might be more receptive to her. But everything about him aroused her passion and sent her into sensory overload.

"Brooke?"

Unable to verbalize the emotions raging through her, she avoided looking at Nic and found the perfect distraction in a waitress's hard stare. The woman had been watching from the kitchen doorway ever since Brooke had sat down. "I don't think that waitress likes me," Brooke commented, indicating the curvaceous brunette. "Did I interrupt something between you two?"

"Natasa? Don't be ridiculous."

His impatient dismissal raised Brooke's spirits slightly. She already knew Nic wasn't the sort to engage in casual encounters. Her five-year pursuit of him had demonstrated that he wasn't ruled by his body's urges.

"She's awfully pretty and hasn't taken her eye off you since I sat down."

"Do you want something to eat?" Nic signaled Natasa and she came over.

"Another beer for me," he told the waitress. "What are you drinking?" He looked to Brooke.

"Water."

"And an order of *taramosalata.*"

"What is that?" Brooke quizzed, her gaze following the generous sway of Natasa's hips as she wound her way back toward the kitchen.

"A spread made from fish roe. You'll like it."

You'll like it.

Did he realize the impact those words had on her nerve endings?

It was what he'd said to her their first night together. To her amazement, once he'd stopped resisting her flirtatious banter and taken the lead, she'd been overcome by his authoritative manner and had surrendered to his every whim. Her skin tingled, remembering the sweep of his fingers across the sensitized planes of her body. He'd made love to her with a thoroughness she'd never known. Not one inch of her body had gone unclaimed by him and she'd let it all happen. Her smile had blazed undiminished for five months until he'd driven up to San Francisco for *the talk*.

Natasa returned with their drinks. She gave Brooke a quick once-over, plunked two bottles on the table and shot Nic a hard look he didn't notice. Brooke grinned as Nic reached for her bottled water and broke the seal without being asked. He didn't know it, but this was just one of the things that had become a ritual with them. During the past five years, Brooke had repeatedly asked him to do her small favors and Nic had obliged, grumbling all the while about her inability to do the simplest tasks. He'd never figured out that each time he helped her, he became a little more invested in their relationship.

Six months ago all her subtle efforts had brought results. After a successful test firing of the *Griffin*'s ignition system, the team had been celebrating in Glen's backyard. Nic had been animated, electrified. She'd been a moth to his flame, basking in his warm smiles and affectionate touches. At the end of the evening he'd meshed their fingers together and drawn her to the privacy of the front porch where he'd kissed her silly.

Lying sleepless in her bed that night she'd relived the mind-blowing kiss over and over and wondered what she'd done to finally break through Nic's resistance. She hadn't been able to pinpoint anything, nor did she think that day's success had been the trigger. The team had enjoyed several triumphs in the previous few months. In the end Brooke had decided her years of flirting had finally begun to reach him.

After that night, she'd noticed a subtle difference in the way Nic behaved toward her and began to hope that he might have finally figured out she was the one for him.

Brooke increased the frequency of her weekend visits to the Mojave Air and Space Port, where the *Griffin* team had their offices. Despite the increased urgency to finish the rocket and get it ready for a test launch, Nic had made time for quiet dinners. Afterward, they'd often talked late into the night. After two months, he'd taken things to the next level. He'd shared not just his body with her, but his dreams and desires, as well. At the time, she'd thought she was getting to know the real Nic. Now she realized how much he'd kept from her.

With fresh eyes, Brooke regarded her brother's best friend and saw only a stranger. In his stylish clothes and expensive shades he looked every inch a rich European. She contemplated the arrogant tilt of his head, the utter command of his presence as he watched her. Why had she never picked up on it earlier?

Because his English was flawlessly Americanized. Because he went to work every day in ordinary jeans and T-shirts. Granted, he filled out his commonplace clothes in an extraordinary manner, but nothing about his impressive pecs and washboard abs screamed aristocracy. She'd always assumed he rarely let off steam with his fellow scientists because he was preoccupied with work.

Now she realized he'd been brought up with different expectations placed upon him than people in her orbit. A picture formed in her mind. Nic, tall and proud, his broad shoulders filling out a formfitting tuxedo, a red sash across his chest from shoulder to hip. He looked regal. Larger than life. Completely out of reach.

Brooke had always believed that people didn't regret the things they did, only the things they didn't. She liked to believe she was richer for every experience she'd had, good or bad. Would she have given her heart to Nic if she'd known who he was from the beginning? Yes. Brief as it had been, she cherished every moment of their time together.

While logic enabled her to rationalize why she couldn't marry him, her heart prevented her from walking away without a backward glance. And she suspected he wasn't thrilled to be sacrificing himself so that his family could continue to reign. As devastating as it was to think she'd have to give up on a future with Nic, wanting to be with him was a yearning she couldn't shake off.

"I'm going to ask you a question," she announced abruptly, her gaze drilling through his bland expression. "And I expect the truth this time."

Nic's beer bottle hung between the table and his lips. "I suppose I owe you that."

"You're darned right you do." She ignored the brief flare of amusement in his eyes. "I want to know the real reason you broke up with me."

"I've already explained the reason. We have no future. I have to go home and I have to marry." He stared at the harbor behind her, his expression chiseled in granite.

She'd obviously phrased her question wrong. "And if your brother hadn't married someone who couldn't have children? Would you have broken things off?"

What she really wanted to know was if he loved her, but she wasn't sure he'd pondered how deep his feelings for her ran. Also, a month ago he'd apparently accepted that he had to marry someone else and it wasn't his nature to dwell on impossibilities.

"It's a simple question," she prompted as the silence stretched. He surely hated being put on the spot like this, but she couldn't move on until she knew.

His chest rose and fell on a huge sigh as he met her gaze with heavy-lidded eyes. Something flickered within those bronze-colored depths. Something that made her stomach contract and her spirits soar.

She'd journeyed to Ithaca to tell him about the baby, but also because she couldn't bear to let him go. Now she understood that she had to. But not yet. She had two days before she had to return to the States. Two days to say goodbye. All she needed was a sign from Nic that he hadn't wanted to give her up.

"No." He spoke the word like a curse. "We'd still be together."

The instant the words left his lips, Nic wished he'd maintained the lies. Brooke's eyes kindled with satisfaction and her body relaxed. She resembled a contented cat. He'd seen the look many times and knew it meant trouble.

"I think we should spend the time between now and when you leave *together*." She gave the last word a specific emphasis that he couldn't misinterpret.

Nic shook his head, vigorously rejecting her suggestion. "That's not fair to you." *Duty. Honor. Integrity.* He repeated the words like a prayer. "I won't take advantage of you that way."

Brooke leaned forward, her gaze sharpening. "Has it ever occurred to you that I like it when you take advantage of me?"

The world beyond their table blurred until it was only him and her and the intense emotional connection that had clicked into place the first time they'd made love, a connection that couldn't be severed.

"I never noticed." His attempt to banter with her so that she'd adopt a less serious mood fell flat.

Her determination gained momentum. "Tell me you don't want to spend your last days of freedom with me."

Every molecule that made up his body screamed at him to agree. "It's not that I don't want to. I shouldn't." He spoke quickly to prevent her from arguing with him. "Ever since finding out I had to return home and get married, I promised myself I wouldn't touch you again."

"That's just silly." She gave him a wicked smile. "You like touching me."

In the time he'd known her, he'd learned just how powerful that smile could be. It had whittled away at his willpower until he'd done the one thing he knew he shouldn't. He'd fallen hard.

Duty. Honor. Integrity. The lament filled his mind. If only Brooke didn't make it so damned hard to do the right thing.

She got up from her chair and stepped into his space.

He tipped his head back and assessed her determined expression. His heart shuddered as she put her palms flat on his shoulders and settled herself on his lap. Even though Nic had braced himself for the arousing pressure of her firm rear on his thighs, it took every bit of concentration he possessed to put his hands behind his back, safely out of range of her tempting curves. What sort of hell had he let himself fall into?

"What do you think you're doing?"

"Are you all right?" she asked, tracing her fingertips across his furrowed brow.

God, she was a tempting lapful.

"I'm fine."

"You don't look fine."

"I'm great, and you didn't answer my question." He pulled her spicy scent into his lungs and held it there. He longed to bury his face in her neck and imprint her upon his senses. "What are you doing on my lap?"

"Demonstrating that you want me as much as I want you."

He hated himself for hoping she'd continue the demonstration until he couldn't catch his breath. Making love to her was amazing. He'd never been with anyone who matched him the way she did. Anticipation gnawed on him like a puppy with a stolen shoe.

"I assure you I want you a great deal more." How he kept his voice so clinical, Nic would never know.

"Then you'll let me stay on the island for the next few days?"

She knew him better than anyone and once she'd discovered his weakness where she was concerned, she'd pressed her advantage at every opportunity. Before they'd made love, she'd slipped past his defenses like a ninja. Now they'd been intimate and he didn't doubt that she would exploit his passion to get her way.

"I left California without saying goodbye because leaving you was so damned hard." When he'd broken off things a month ago, he'd been lucky to escape before her shock at his announcement wore off. Ending their relationship was one of the hardest things he'd ever done. If she'd begged him to stay, he wasn't sure if he could have done the right thing by Sherdana. "Nothing good will come of putting off the inevitable."

"The way you disappeared left me feeling anxious and out of sorts. I understood that we'd broken up, but what I didn't get was how you could take off without saying anything. You should have explained your circumstances. I could have processed the situation and gotten closure. That's what I need now. A few days to say goodbye properly."

"And by properly you mean…?"

Her serious expression dissolved into one of unabashed mischief. "A few days of incredible sex and unbridled passion should do it."

How could any man resist such an offer? Visions of her flat on her back with his hands skimming along her soft, delectable curves rose to torture him. A smile and a frown played tug-of-war on his face. But this was not the time to stop listening to the voice inside his head that reminded him he had to give her up. The smartest thing would be to avoid making more memories that would haunt him the rest of his life.

"Don't you think it would be better if we didn't let ourselves indulge in something that has no future?"

"I'm not going to pretend we have a future. I'm going to cherish every moment of our time together with the knowledge that in the end we'll say goodbye forever." She slid her fingers into his hair. Her thumbs traced the outline of his ears. "I can see you need more convincing, so I'm going to kiss you."

He drank in the scent of honey and vanilla rising off her skin, knowing she tasted as good as she smelled. Her generous lips, rosy and bare of lipstick, parted in anticipation of the promised kiss. Nothing would make him happier than to spend the rest of his life enjoying the curve and texture of her lips. The way she sighed as he kissed her. The soft hitch in her breath as he grazed her lower lip with his teeth.

A tremor transmitted her agitation to him. He longed to inspire more such trembling. To revisit her most ticklish spots, the erogenous zones that made her moan. With erotic impulses twisting his nerves into knots, Nic snagged her gaze. Silver flecks ringed her irises, growing brighter as she stared at his mouth. His pulse thundered in his ears as the moment stretched without a kiss coming anywhere near his lips.

"Damn it, Brooke."

He would not scoop the wayward strand of hair behind her tiny ear and let his knuckles linger against her flushed cheek. He refused to tug on her braid and coax her lips close enough to drift over his.

"What's the matter, Nic?" Her fingers explored his eyebrows and tested his lashes.

Duty. Honor. Integrity. The litany was starting to lose its potency.

"In less than a week I'll never see you again." He locked his hands together behind his back. Tremors began in his arm muscles.

"I know." She switched her attention to his mouth. Her long, red lashes cast delicate shadows on her cheeks.

Heat surged into his face. Hell, heat filled every nook and cranny of his body. Especially where her heart-shaped rear end rested. How could she help but notice his aroused state?

"We'd only be prolonging the inevitable," he reminded her, unsure why he was holding out when he wanted so badly to agree to her mad scheme.

"I need this. I need you." She stroked her thumb against his lower lip. "An hour. A day. A week. I'll take whatever I can get."

Nic counted his heartbeats to avoid focusing on the emotions raging through him. The need to crush her in his arms would overwhelm him any second. Denying himself her compassion and understanding in the days following the accident hadn't been easy, but at the time he'd known that he had to return to Sherdana. Just because Brooke now knew what was going on didn't give him permission to stop acting honorably.

He wasn't prepared for the air she blew in his ear. His body jerked in surprise, and he sucked in a sharp breath. "Stop that."

"You didn't like it?" Laughter gave her voice a husky quality.

"You know perfectly well I did," he murmured hoarsely. "Our food is going to be here any second. Perhaps you should return to your own seat."

"I'm here for a kiss and a kiss is what I'm going to get." She was enjoying this far too much. And, damn it, so was he.

With a fatalistic sigh, Nic accepted that he'd let himself

be drawn too far into her game to turn back. As much as he wanted to savor the expressions flitting across her face, he stared at the fishing boats bobbing near the cement seawall. Alert to her slightest movement, he felt the tingle on his cheek an instant before her lips grazed his skin.

"Let's stop all the foreplay, shall we," he finally said.

"Oh, all right. Spoilsport. I was enjoying having you at my mercy. But if you insist."

Lightning danced in her eyes. She secured his face between her hands and grazed her lips across his.

"Again." His voice was half demand, half plea. He hardened his will and inserted steel into his tone. "And this time put a little effort into it."

"Whatever you say."

He let his lashes drop as her mouth drifted over his again. This time she applied more pressure, a little more technique. As kisses went, it was pretty chaste, but her little hum of pleasure tipped his world on its axis. And when she nibbled on his lip, murmuring in Italian, desire incinerated his resistance.

"Benedette le voci tante ch'io chiamando il nome de mia donna ò sparte, e i sospiri, et le lagrime, e 'l desio."

How was he supposed to resist a woman with a PhD in Italian literature? Although he knew what she'd said, he wanted to hear her speak the words again.

"Translation?"

"And blessed be all of the poetry I scattered, calling out my lady's name, and all the sighs, and tears, and the passion."

"Italian love poetry?" he groused, amused in spite of the lust raking him with claws dipped in the sweetest aphrodisiac.

"It seemed appropriate." Her fingers splaying over his rapidly beating heart, she swooped in for one last kiss before getting to her feet. "I think I made my point." With a satisfied smirk, she returned to her chair.

"What point?"

"That we both could use closure."

Over the course of the kiss he'd grasped what she wanted to do, but he'd worked diligently over the past month to come to grips with living without her and couldn't imagine reopening himself to the loss all over again. And she'd just demonstrated he'd never survive a few days let alone a week in her company. He'd be lucky if he made it past the next hours. No. She had to go. And go soon. Because if she didn't, he'd give in and make love to her. And that would be disastrous.

"I got my closure a month ago when I broke things off," he lied. "But I understand that I've sprung a lot of information on you today that you'll want to assimilate. Stay for a couple days."

"As friends?" She sounded defeated.

"It's for the best."

Four

The discussion before lunch dampened Brooke's spirits and left her in a thoughtful mood as she ate her way through a plate of moussaka, and followed that up with yogurt and honey for dessert. Nic, never one for small talk, seemed content with the silence, but he watched her through half-lidded eyes.

Telling him she was pregnant had just become a lot more complicated. As had her decision regarding the teaching position at Berkeley. Before Nic had broken it off with her a month ago she'd been confident that he was her future and she'd chosen him over her ideal job. When he left she should have returned to her original career path, but finding out that she was pregnant had created a whole new group of variables.

Gone was her fantasy that once Nic heard he was going to be a father, he would return to California and they would live happily ever after as a family. Since that wasn't going to happen, the Berkeley job was back on the table. Brooke wished she could summon up the enthusiasm she'd once felt at the possibility of teaching there.

And then there were the challenges that came with being a single mom. If she moved back to LA she would be close to her parents and they would be thrilled to help.

Thanks to Nic's revelations she was a bundle of indecisiveness. They returned to Nic's car for the ride back to the villa. He told her he would have Elena's husband, Thasos, return the boat later. As the car swept along the narrow road circling Kioni's tranquil bay, Brooke felt her anxiety rise and fall with each curve.

From this vantage point, halfway up the side of the scrubby hills that made up the island's landscape, she could see beyond the harbor to the azure water of the Ionian Sea. Glen had described Ithaca as a pile of rocks with scrubby brush growing here and there, but he'd done the picturesque landscape a disservice.

"We'll be to my house in ten minutes." Nic pointed toward a spot on the hill where a bit of white was visible among the green hillside.

In the short time she'd been here, Brooke had fallen in love with Nic's villa. It made her curious about the rest of his family and the life they lived in Sherdana. Did they live in a palace? She tried to picture Nic growing up in a fussy, formal place with hundreds of rooms and dozens of servants.

As the villa disappeared from view around another bend, Brooke glanced over her shoulder and estimated the distance back to the village. Two or three miles. The car turned off the main road and rolled down a long driveway that angled toward the edge of the cliff. When first the extensive gardens and then the house came into view, she caught her breath.

"This is beautiful," she murmured, certain her compliment wasn't effusive enough. "I didn't see this side of the house earlier."

"Gabriel found the place. We bought it for our eighteenth birthday. I'm afraid I haven't used it much."

Built on a hillside overlooking the bay, the home was actually a couple buildings connected together by terraces and paths. Surrounded by cypress and olive trees, the stucco buildings with the terra-cotta tile roofs sprawled on the hillside, their gardens spread around them like skirts.

The nearby hills had been planted with cosmos, heather and other native flowering plants to maintain a natural look. A cluster of small terra-cotta pots, containing bright pink and lavender flowers greeted visitors at the door. A large clay urn had been tipped on its side in the center of the grouping to give the display some height and contrast.

Nic stopped the car. Shutting off the engine, he turned to face her, one hand resting on the seat behind her head. The light breeze blew a strand of hair across her face. Before Brooke could deal with it, Nic's fingers drifted along her cheek and pushed it behind her ear. She half shut her eyes against the delight that surged in her. Her stomach turned a cartwheel as she spied the thoughtful half smile curving his lips. Nic's smile was like drinking brandy. It warmed her insides and stimulated her senses.

"Maybe tomorrow I can show you the windmills," he said, his gaze drifting over her face. The fondness in his eyes made her chest tighten.

"Sure." Her voice had developed a disconcerting croak. She cleared her throat. "I'd like that."

She let out an enormous yawn while Nic was unlocking the front door. He raised his eyebrows and she clapped her hand over her mouth.

"I see you didn't take my advice earlier about getting some sleep."

"I was too wound up. Now I'm having trouble keeping my eyes open. Feel like joining me for a nap?"

Only a minute widening of his eyes betrayed Nic's reaction to her offer. "From what you've told me I have a bunch of emails to answer. I'll catch up with you before dinner."

All too familiar with Nic's substantial willpower, Brooke retreated to the terrace where she'd first found him. In the harbor a hundred feet below, the water was an incredible cerulean blue, the color accentuated by the tile roofs of the houses that lined the wharf and scaled the steep verdant green hills cupping the horseshoe-shaped harbor.

She rested her hands on the stone wall and pondered the nature of fate. Before she'd met Nic, she'd been pursued by any number of men who were ready to do what it took to win her affection. But instead of falling for one of them, she'd chosen a man who was far more interested in his rocket ship than her. All the while, she'd hoped that maybe his enthusiasm for his work could somehow translate into passion for her.

The explosive chemistry between her and Nic had seemed like a foundation they could build a relationship on. The way he'd dropped his guard and given her a glimpse of his emotions had left her breathless with hope that maybe his big-brother act had been his way of protecting his heart. Thanks to all her previous romantic escapades that Glen was only too happy to bring up over and over, Nic had regarded her as a bit of a loose cannon when it came to love.

Brooke turned her back on the view. She had a lot to think about. Following Nic to this island had proved way more interesting and enlightening than she'd expected.

While she'd only been his best friend's little sister, it hurt that neither man trusted her with the truth. She didn't blame Glen for keeping Nic's confidences. Her brother wouldn't have been the amazing man he'd been without his honorable side. But she could, and did, blame Nic for keeping her in the dark.

For five years he'd kept some enormous secrets from her. That knowledge stung. But now she had a secret of her own. Given what she now knew about Nic, what was her best course of action?

Despite her exhaustion after being awake for twenty-four hours, she paced, the sound of her sandals slapping against the stone of the terrace breaking the tranquil silence. Seeing Nic, kissing him and finding out that he was not the hardworking scientist she'd always known but a prince of some country she'd only heard of in passing, had her thoughts in a frenetic whirl.

And then there was the big question of the day. The one she'd been avoiding for the past hour. Was she going to tell Nic about her pregnancy?

In the wake of all she'd learned, was it fair to tell him he was going to be a father? He couldn't marry her even if he'd wanted to. Nor would they be living on the same continent. Being the prince of a small European country meant he would be under the keenest scrutiny. Would he even want to acknowledge an illegitimate child? Yet was it fair to deny him the opportunity to make that decision?

Her best friend, Theresa, would help her answer some of these questions. She was the most sensible and grounded person in Brooke's life. Brooke went down to the guesthouse, retrieved her phone from the bed where she'd left it and dialed Theresa's number.

"Well, it's about time you called me back," Theresa started, sounding more like Brooke's mother than her best friend. "I've left you, like, four messages."

Brooke tried to shrug away the tension in her shoulders, but that was hard when she was braced against an onslaught of lecturing. "Five, actually. I'm sorry I didn't call sooner—"

"You know I'm just worried about you. The last time we talked, you were going to get your brother to tell you where Nic had gone."

"I did that."

"So where is he?"

"About two miles down the road from the most gorgeous Greek town you've ever seen."

"And you know this Greek town is so gorgeous because…?" Theresa's voice held a hint of alarm.

"I've seen it."

"Brooke, no."

"Yep."

A long pause followed. Brooke almost wished she was there to watch her best friend's expression fluctuate from annoyed to incredulous and back again.

"What about the Berkeley interview?"

"It's in three days."

"Are you going to make it back in time?"

In truth she wasn't sure she wanted to. The idea of raising a baby by herself scared her. She wanted to be close to family and that meant living in LA. "That's my intention."

"What was Nic's reaction when you showed up?"

"He was pretty surprised to see me."

"And when you told him about the baby?"

Panic and longing surged through her in confusing, conflicting waves. Twenty-four hours earlier, coming to find him had felt necessary instead of reckless or impulsive. And in hindsight, it had been foolishly optimistic. She'd been convinced Nic would return to California with her once he knew he was going to be a father.

"I haven't yet."

"What are you waiting for?"

Brooke fell back on the bed and stared at the ceiling. "Things got a little complicated after I got here."

"Did you sleep with him again?"

"No." She paused to smile. "Not yet."

"Brooke, you are my best friend and I want nothing but the best for you," Theresa began in overly patient tones. "But you need to realize if he wanted to be with you he would."

"It's not as simple as that." Or was it? Hadn't Nic chosen duty to his country over her? Once again Brooke pictured Nic in formal attire, standing between two other men who looked just like him. Beside them were two thrones where an older couple wearing crowns sat in regal splendor. "But he cares about me. It's just that he's in a complicated situation. And I couldn't tell him over the phone that I'm pregnant."

"Okay. I'll give you that." Theresa was making an effort to be positive and supportive, but clearly she didn't believe that Brooke's actions were wise. "But you chased him all the way to Greece. And now you haven't told him. So what's wrong?"

"What makes you think anything is wrong?"

"Gee, I don't know. We've been best friends since third grade. I think I can tell when something's bothering you. What's going on?" Theresa's voice softened. "Is he doing okay?"

As long as the two girls had known each other, Theresa never understood Brooke's restless longing for the drama of romance. The thrill of flirting. The heart-pounding excitement of falling in love. Married to a man she'd dated since college, Theresa was completely and happily settled. Safe with a reliable husband. And although Theresa would never say it out loud, Brooke always felt as if her friend judged her because she wanted more.

"Physically yes, unless you count hungover. He looked terrible when I showed up this morning."

"So, he's really taking the accident hard."

"Of course he is. He and Glen have been obsessed with

this dream of theirs for five long years. And as you said, he blames himself for what happened." Brooke's breath came out in a ragged sigh as her reaction to what she'd learned finally caught up with her. "He's not coming back."

"Sure he is. If anyone can convince him to not give up it's you."

"I can't. There's a bunch of other things going on."

"What kind of other things?"

"Turns out there are problems at home and he has to go back and marry someone."

"What?" Theresa screeched. "He's engaged?"

"Not yet, but he will be soon."

"Soon? How soon? Does he have a girlfriend he's going to propose to? Is that why he broke your heart?"

"No." Brooke knew she wasn't being clear, but was having a hard time explaining what she still struggled to grasp. "Nothing so simple. Theresa, he's a prince."

Silence. "I'm sorry, a what?"

"A prince." Her reaction was beginning to settle in. Brooke swiped away a sudden rush of tears as her ears picked up nothing but the hiss of air through the phone's speaker. "Are you still there?"

"Yes, I'm here, but this damned international call has gone wonky. Can you repeat what you said."

"Nic is a prince. He's second in line to the throne of a small European country called Sherdana."

Her breath evened out as she waited out her best friend's stupefaction. It wouldn't last long. Theresa was one of the most pragmatic people she knew. It was part of what kept them friends for so long. Opposites attract. Theresa needed Brooke's particular variety of crazy to shake up her life, and Brooke relied on Theresa's common sense to keep her grounded.

"You're kidding me, right? This whole phone call is some sort of setup for one of those wacky reality shows

where people get punked or filmed doing stupid things."
She paused and waited for Brooke to fill in an affirmative.
When Brooke remained silent Theresa sighed and said,
"Okay, you'd better give it to me from the top."

Nic sat in the small den off the living room, his laptop on the love seat beside him, his thoughts lingering on
Brooke and her crazy notion that they should say goodbye and gain closure by spending the next few days in bed
together. Had he done a good enough job convincing her
that wasn't going to happen when he desperately wanted
to make love to her again? During their five months together, she'd learned all she had to do was crook a finger
and he was happy to abandon his work in favor of spending hours in her arms. Nic growled as he pondered his
susceptibility to her abundant charms. He was fighting a
battle with himself and with her. In a few hours she would
return, refreshed and ready for the next skirmish and he'd
better have his defenses reinforced.

With a snort of disgust, Nic turned on the computer in
the den and cued up his email. She'd claimed there were
dozens of unanswered emails, but the inbox was empty. It
took him fifteen minutes to find them among the folders
where he shunted the messages he didn't wish to delete
and restore the settings to the way he liked them. Brooke
was a disaster when it came to anything involving technology. Glen had found his sister's deficiency funny and
endearing. Nic just found it exasperating. Like so many
other things about her.

She was always late. In fact, her sense of time was so
skewed that if he needed her to be somewhere, he usually
built in a cushion of thirty minutes. Then there was her inability to say no to anyone. This usually led to her getting
involved in something she needed to be bailed out of. Like
at *Griffin*'s annual team picnic when she'd agreed to take

all the kids for a nature hike and then got lost. It had taken Nic and Glen, plus a half dozen concerned parents, to find them. Of course, the kids all thought it was the best adventure they'd ever been on. Brooke had kept them calm and focused, never letting them know how much trouble they were in. Later, when he'd scolded her for worrying everyone, she'd simply shrugged her shoulders and pointed out that nothing bad had happened. She just didn't think about the consequences of her actions. And that drove him crazy.

As crazy as the way she leveraged her lean, toned body to incite his baser instincts. Whenever she took a weekend break from school and came to visit, he found it impossible to concentrate on the *Griffin* project. She hung out in his office, alternating between cajoling and pouting until she paid attention to her. Most days he held out because eventually she'd grow tired of the game and let him get back to work. Unfortunately before that happened, he had to endure her flirtatious hugs and seemingly innocent body brushes. Usually by the time she headed back to San Francisco on Sunday afternoon, he was aroused, off schedule and in a savage mood.

His phone rang. Gabriel. The first in line to the throne sounded relaxed and a touch smug as he passed along the message Nic had been dreading.

"Mother is sending the jet to pick you up the day after tomorrow and wants to know what time you can be at the airport."

"What's so urgent? I thought I had over a week until your wedding."

"She has a series of parties and events leading up to the big day that you and Christian will be expected to attend. From what I understand she has compiled quite a list of potential brides for you two to fight over."

And so it began. Nic's thoughts turned toward the woman napping in the guesthouse. His heart wrenched at the thought of being parted from her so soon after reconnecting. She would be disappointed to find out their time would be cut short, but he had warned her.

"Are any of these women…?" What was he trying to ask? Without meeting any of them, he'd already decided they were unacceptable. None of them were Brooke.

"Beautiful? Smart? Wealthy? What?"

"Am I going to *like* any of them?" As soon as the question was out Nic felt foolish.

"I'm sure you're going to like all of them. You just have to figure out which one you can see yourself spending the rest of your life with." Gabriel's words and tone were matter-of-fact.

"Is that how you felt when you first started poring over the candidates?"

Gabriel paused before answering. "Not exactly. I had Olivia in mind from the first."

"But you spent a year considering and meeting possible matches. Why do that if you already knew who you wanted?"

"Two reasons. Because Mother would not have accepted that I had already met the perfect girl and at the time only my subconscious realized Olivia was the one."

Nic wished he was having this conversation face-to-face because his brother's expression would provide clues mere words lacked. "You've lost me."

"As I worked my way through the list, I realized I compared each woman I met to Olivia."

"She was your ideal."

"She was the one I wanted."

The conviction throbbing in Gabriel's low voice spurred Nic to envy his brother for the first time since they were kids. Before Nic had discovered his passion for science and engineering, he'd wondered what contribution he could make to the country. Gabriel would rule. All Christian cared about was having fun and shirking responsibility. Nic had wanted to have a positive effect on the world. A lofty ambition for an eight-year-old.

Gabriel continued speaking, "Only I resented my duty to marry and didn't know how perfect Olivia was for me. Even when I proposed to her I was blind to my heart's true desire. Thank goodness my instincts weren't hampered by my hardheadedness."

"At what point did you figure out you'd selected the perfect woman?"

"The night my girls came to stay at the palace. Olivia took them under her wing and zealously guarded them from anyone she believed might upset them. Me included." He chuckled. "And she never wavered in her love for them, not even when she thought I was still in love with their mother."

"And speaking of Karina and Bethany, how are your girls?"

"Growing more beautiful and more terrifying by the week. Thank goodness they adore Olivia or they'd be terrorizing the palace staff a lot more than they do. Somehow she guides their energy into positive channels and makes the whole process look effortless. No one else can manage them without being ready to pull their hair out."

"Not even Mother?"

"At first, but now they realize she is too fond of them to scold. Father indulges their appetite for sweets and Ariana has shown them every good hiding place the palace has to offer."

"It's not called the terrible twos for nothing."

"You'll see soon enough. I'll have the plane pick you up tomorrow around noon."

"Fine." That should give him time to make sure Brooke was safely on a plane heading for home.

"See that you're there on time."

"Where else would I be? I have nowhere to go but home."

Nic ended the call with a weary sigh and mulled what Gabriel had said about his search for a wife. That his brother had settled on the perfect woman before his quest had even begun didn't lessen Nic's unease over what was to come. Already his mind and body had chosen the woman for him. She was currently stretched out on the bed in the guesthouse. If he was anything like Gabriel, he was going to have an impossible time finding anyone who could match her perfect imperfection.

Several hours later, he was opening a bottle of Sherdana's best Pinot Negro to let it breathe when Brooke sailed into the living room. She'd changed clothes again. The tail of her pastel tied-dyed kimono fluttered behind her as she walked, exposing a mint-green crocheted tank and the ruffled hem of her leg-baring floral shorts.

A light breeze swept in from the terrace and plucked at her dark copper curls. She'd loosened her hair from its braid and it flowed in rich waves over her shoulders and down her back. She stroked a lock away from her lips. He caught himself staring at her and shifted his attention back to the wine.

How often in the past five years had he longed to sink his fingers into her tempestuous red locks and lose himself in the chaotic tangle? He'd imagined the texture would feel like the finest Chinese silk sliding along his bare chest. He'd been right.

Nic extended a glass of wine toward her. She shook her head.

"Something nonalcoholic if you have it."

He found a container of orange juice and poured her a glass. She sipped at it, her eyes smiling at him over the edge of the glass. Expecting a whole new round of verbal fencing, Nic was surprised when she said, "You mentioned that your sister paints here. Could I see her studio?"

"Sure."

He led the way onto the terrace and around the villa in the opposite direction of the guesthouse. A small building with broad windows facing north sat on a little rise overlooking the harbor mouth. Nic unlocked the door and gestured for Brooke to go inside.

"Oh, these are all wonderful," she said the minute she walked in.

Though Brooke was always generous with her praise, Nic thought she was going a little overboard in talking about Ariana's work. Nic was proud of what his sister had accomplished with her paintings but didn't really get her modern style. She had often accused him of being stuck in the Middle Ages in terms of his taste. Brooke, on the other hand, seemed to get exactly what his sister was trying to do.

He enjoyed watching her stroll through his sister's art studio and study each canvas in turn, treating every painting like a masterpiece. By the time Brooke returned to where he stood just inside the door, her delighted grin had Nic smiling, as well. The next time he saw Ariana, he would be sure to tell her what an accomplished artist she was.

"I never looked at Ariana's art that way before," Nic said as he relocked the studio and escorted Brooke back toward the main house. "Thank you for opening my eyes."

She looked caught off guard by his compliment. "You're welcome."

At that moment Nic realized how rarely he'd ever offered Brooke any encouragement or a reason to believe he appreciated her. How had she stayed so relentlessly positive as he'd thrown one obstacle after another in her path? All she'd ever asked was for him to like her and treat her with civility. Was it her fault that she agitated his emotions and incited his hormones?

"What are you thinking about?" she asked as they stepped back into the main house. She gathered her hair into a twist and secured it into a topknot.

"Regrets. I spent so much time keeping you at bay."

Again he'd startled her. "You did, but to be fair, I am a little overwhelming."

"And very distracting. I had a hard time concentrating when you were around."

She narrowed her eyes. "Why are you being so nice to me all of a sudden?"

"I had a call from my brother while you were resting and I have to leave for Sherdana the day after tomorrow."

"So soon?" Her lips curved downward.

Nic wanted to put his arms around her, but it would do neither of them any good to deepen their connection when the time to part was so near. "Apparently my mother has planned several events she'd like me to attend in the next week, culminating in Gabriel and Olivia's wedding."

"But I thought they were already married."

"They are. Actually…" Nic stared out the window at Kioni in the distance. "He brought her to Ithaca for a surprise wedding ceremony."

"That's very romantic."

"And unlike Gabriel to put his desires before the needs of the country. But he's crazy about Olivia and couldn't bear to live without her."

Something about Brooke's silence caught his attention. She was staring at the floor lost in thought. "So why are they getting married again?"

"The crown prince's wedding is pretty momentous and my parents decided it was better to have a second ceremony than to rob the citizens of the celebration. There will be parties every night leading up to the big event, both at the palace and venues around our capital city of Carone."

"Tell me about the parties at the palace. They must be formal affairs." Brooke's smile bloomed. "Do you have to dance?"

"Only when I can't avoid it."

"So you know how."

"It's part of every prince's training," he intoned, mimicking his dance teacher's severe manner. "I don't have Gabriel's technique or Christian's flair, but I don't step on my partner's toes anymore."

"After dinner tonight you are going to dance with me." She held up a hand when he began to protest. "Don't argue. I remember on three separate occasions when you told me you had no idea how to dance."

"No," he corrected her. "I told you I don't dance. There's a difference."

"Semantics."

"Very well." He knew that taking her in his arms and swaying with her to soft music would lead to trouble. But he could teach her a Sherdanian country dance. The movements were energetic and the only touching required was hand to hand. "After dinner."

"So what are we having that smells so delicious?"

"Elena left us lamb stew and salad for dinner."

Brooke drifted to the stove where a pot simmered on a low flame. "I don't know how I can be hungry after all we ate for lunch, but suddenly I'm starved."

Something about the way she said the word made him grind his teeth. She was hungry for food, but the groan in her voice made him hungry for something else entirely. Directing her toward the refrigerator where Elena had put the salad, he spooned the stew into bowls and tried not to remember Brooke beneath him in bed, her red hair fanned across his pillow, lips curved in lazy satisfaction.

"Can I help?"

He handed her a bowl and a basket of bread, almost pushing it at her in an effort to keep her at bay.

She walked toward the table. "I love the bread here in Greece. That and the desserts. I could live on them."

"I hope you like the stew, as well. Elena is an excellent cook."

"I'm sure it's wonderful."

Nic's housekeeper had set the table earlier so there was little left to do but sit down and enjoy the meal. The patch of late-afternoon sunlight on the tile floor had advanced a good three feet by the time they finished eating. Following his example, Brooke had torn pieces of the fresh-baked bread and dipped them into the stew. He'd lost count how many times her tongue came out to catch a crumb on her lip or a spot of gravy at the corner of her mouth.

For dessert Elena had left baklava, a sticky, sweet concoction made of stacked sheets of phyllo dough spread with butter, sugar, nuts and honey. He couldn't wait to watch Brooke suck the sticky honey from her fingers.

And she didn't disappoint him.

"What's so funny?" she demanded, her tongue darting out to clean the corner of her mouth.

Nic banked a groan and sipped his wine. "I'm trying to remember the last time I enjoyed a pan of baklava this much."

"You haven't had any."

He imagined drizzling honey on her skin and following the trail with his tongue. The bees in Greece made thick sweet honey he couldn't get enough of. Against her skin it would be heaven. The arousal that had taunted him all through the meal now exploded with fierce determination. Nic sat back in his chair all too aware of the tightness in his pants and the need clawing at him.

"You've enjoyed it enough for both of us."

"It was delicious." Cutting another piece, she held it out. "Sure you don't want some?"

The question was innocent enough, but the light in her gray-green eyes as she peered at him from beneath her lashes was anything but. Avoiding her gaze, he shook his head.

"As much as I'm enjoying your attempt to seduce me, I'm afraid my intentions toward you haven't changed."

"We'll see." Resolve replaced flirtation in her eyes. She sat back and assessed him. "I still have two nights and a day to dishonor you."

Eager to avoid further banter, he cleared the plates from the table and busied himself putting away the remnants of the stew.

"I can hear what you're thinking," Brooke murmured, following him to the sink. "You're thinking it took me five years to wear you down the first time." She set the pan of baklava on the counter and swept a finger over a patch of honey. "But have you considered that I know a little bit more about what turns you on after all the nights we spent together?"

Out of the corner of his eye Nic watched, his mouth dry, as she stuck her finger into her mouth, closed her eyes in rapt delight and licked off the honey. She was killing him.

"Two nights and a day, Nic." She said again. "Hours and hours of glorious, delirious pleasure as we explore every inch of each other and get lost in deep slow kisses."

But he wasn't free to have the sort of fun Brooke suggested. And one way or another, he intended to make her understand.

"And then what?" he demanded, his voice more curt than he'd intended.

She blinked. "What do you mean?"

"What happens after the fun?" While hot water ran into the sink, he propped his hip against the counter and crossed his arms. "Have you thought about what happens when we leave this island and go our separate ways?"

Her shoulders sagged. "I head back to California and my dream job."

"And I start looking for a wife." To his surprise, he'd managed to get the last word in.

Deciding to capitalize on his advantage, he scrounged up the CD with Sherdanian folk music Ariana had given him for his birthday several years earlier. As the first notes filled the air, he extended his hand in Brooke's direction. "Get over here. It's time for you to learn a traditional Sherdanian country dance."

Five

Nic woke to the smell of coffee and tickle of something in his ear. He reached up to brush away the irritation and heard a soft chuckle. The mattress behind him dipped. His eyes flew open as a hand drifted over his shoulder and a pair of lips slid into the erogenous zone behind his earlobe.

"You sleep like the dead," Brooke murmured. "I have been taking advantage of you for the last fifteen minutes."

"I doubt that." But oh, the idea that she might have hastened his body's awakening.

"Don't be so sure." She sounded awfully damned confident as she snuggled onto the bed behind him, a thin sheet the only barrier between them as she traced the curve of his backside with her knee, running it down along the back of his thigh. As if this caress wasn't provocative enough, she wiggled her pelvis against his butt, aligning her delicious curves against his back from heel to shoulders. "I know you're not wearing any underwear."

"You're guessing."

"Am not." Her palm drifted along his arm, riding the curve of his biceps. Her touch wasn't sexual; she was more like a sculptor admiring a fine marble statue. "I peeked."

He couldn't even gather enough breath to object. What the hell was she doing to him? Reminded of her threat the night before, Nic knew that letting her get her fill of touching him would only lead to further frustration on his part and more boldness on hers. Yet, he couldn't prevent his curiosity from seeing how far she intended to go.

"How long have you been awake?" he asked as her fingers stole up his neck and into his hair. He closed his eyes and savored the soothing caress.

"A couple hours. I went for a swim, started the coffee and grew bored with my own company, so I decided it was time to wake you. How am I doing?"

Brat.

"I'm fully awake," he growled. "Thank you. Now, why don't you run along and fix breakfast while I take a shower."

"Want some company?"

Her mouth opened in a wet kiss on his shoulder. Nic bit back a curse. The swirl of her tongue on his skin caused his hips to twitch. The erection he'd been trying to ignore grew painfully hard.

"Didn't we come to an understanding last night about this being a bad idea?"

"That was your opinion," she corrected. "I think we wasted a perfectly lovely night dancing around your living room when we could have set fire to this big bed of yours."

"Set fire?" Amusement momentarily clouded his desire to roll her beneath him and make her come over and over. She had the damnedest knack for tickling his funny bone.

"Set fire. Tear up the sheets."

He shifted onto his back so he could see her face. Bare of makeup, lips soft with invitation, eyes shadowed by long reddish lashes, her beauty stopped his breath. He cupped her pale cheek in his palm while his heart contracted in remorse. For five months he'd savored the notion of spending the rest of his life with her. He'd claimed her body and given her his heart. At the time, with Gabriel's wedding to Olivia fast approaching and the future of Sherdana safely in their hands, Nic believed he could at last have the life he wanted with the woman who made him happy. It wasn't fair that circumstances had interfered with his plans for the future, but that's the way it was.

His hand fell away from her soft skin. "You know we can't do this."

"Damn it, Nic."

The next thing he knew, she'd straddled him. Astonished by her swift attack and trapped between her strong, supple thighs, Nic reached for the pillow behind his head and dug his fingers in. The challenge in her green-gray gaze helped him maintain control—barely. She settled her hot center firmly over his erection and smirked as his hips lifted off the mattress to meet her partway. She obviously intended to push him past his limits. To incite him to act. He clenched his teeth and held himself immobile.

She put her palms on his chest and leaned forward. "I'm sad and I hate feeling this way. I want to be blissfully happy for just a little while. To forget about the future and just live in the moment."

Where she touched him, he burned. The curtain of her hair swung forward. Still damp from her swim, it brushed against his cheek. He gathered a handful and gently tugged.

"It's not that I don't want that, too," he began and stopped. She couldn't know that what he felt for her went way beyond physical attraction. "I just can't see where that's going to be good for either of us."

Her hands stalked from his chest to his stomach. His muscles twitched in reaction to her touch, betraying him.

He grit his teeth and focused on something less tantalizing than the slender thighs bracketing his hips or the heat of her burning into him through layers of cotton. Unfortunately with her current position, she dominated his field of vision.

"Is that my shirt?"

The last time he'd seen the white button-down, she'd been driving away from his house after they spent the night together. In his eagerness to get her naked the evening before, he'd torn the delicate fabric of her blouse and rendered the garment unwearable. Today, where her damp hair touched the fabric, transparent patches bloomed on her shoulder and chest.

"It is. Every time I wear it I think about you and the nights we spent together."

Nic gripped the bedsheets, endeavoring to stay true to his word and keep his hands off her. Even if his position didn't lend itself to a series of casual affairs, leaving a trail of broken hearts in his wake was not his style. On the other hand, he didn't need the sort of complication a romance with Brooke would bring to his life right now. But since yesterday afternoon he'd become obsessed with all the ways he could touch her without using his hands, and since she'd arrived, he hadn't brooded over the accident for more than five minutes.

"Tell me about the women who are dying to become your princess," she said in a tone as dry as the California desert near the airport test facility. "Are they all beautiful and rich?"

"Do you really want to talk about this?"

"Not really." Her fingers tickled up his sides toward his armpits.

In an effort to stop her before she made him squirm, Nic snagged her wrists and rolled her over. She ended up beneath him, her legs tangled in the sheets. Now that she was trapped in a web of her own making, this was his chance to escape. He should have immediately shifted away from her and put a safe distance between them, but her expression took on a look of such vulnerability that he was transfixed. Pressed chest to groin, they stared at each other.

"Touch me," she whispered, digging her fingers into his biceps.

He flexed his spine, driving his hips tight into hers. She shifted beneath him, rubbing her body against his in a tension-filled rhythm. A groan ripped from his throat as her heat called to him. Today she smelled like pink grapefruit, stimulating with a sweet bitterness. His mouth watered.

"I promised I wouldn't."

"Then, kiss me. You didn't promise not to do that."

That would be following the letter of the law instead of the intent. "You should have been a lawyer," he groused, surrendering to what they both wanted.

His lips lowered to hers. She opened for him like a rose on a warm summer afternoon. He kept the pace slow, concentrating on her mouth while ruthlessly suppressing the urgent thrumming in his groin. Her heart beat in time with his until Nic wasn't sure where he left off and she began. Time was suspended. The room fell away. There was only the softness of her skin beneath his lips, her soft sighs and the growing tension in his body.

This deviation from his intention wouldn't benefit either of them, but he'd grown sick to death of thinking in terms of what he couldn't do, what didn't work, what he stood to lose. He wanted to take joy in this moment and put the future on hold. Brooke had offered him a gift with no strings attached. He would face a lifetime of limits and restrictions soon enough. Why not go wild for a few minutes? Enjoy this exhilarating, vivacious woman who brought joy and laughter into his stolid existence. Who confounded him with her sassy attitude and liberated his emotions. For five years he'd fought against falling for her, afraid if he let her in he might one day have to leave her.

And he'd been right. No sooner had he risked his heart than he'd been forced to make a terrible choice.

"See, that wasn't so hard," she murmured as he broke off the kiss to trail his lips down her neck to the madly beating pulse in her throat.

"I've never met anyone like you. No one knocks me off my game faster."

"It's my dazzling personality."

"It's your damned stubbornness. If Berkeley doesn't work out, you could always teach seminars to salesmen on the art of not taking no for an answer."

Her rock hard nipples burned his chest through the thin cloth, branding him with each impassioned breath she took.

"Unbutton your shirt."

She hesitated at his demand as if unsure what his change of mind might mean. After a long moment, she raised her hands and slipped the first button free. As the top curve of her breast came into view, he lowered his head and tasted her skin. Her gasp made him smile. What he intended to do next would render her breathless.

"Another."

She obliged. He nudged into the ever-widening V, grazing her sensitive skin with the stubble on his chin. A shudder captured her. Nic smiled.

"Keep going."

She unbuttoned the next two buttons in rapid succession, but held on to the edges of the shirt, keeping the material closed. Sensing what he wanted, she peered at him from beneath her lashes. Nic eyed the pink tone in her cheeks.

"Spread the shirt open. I want to look at you."

"Nic, this is—" She broke off as he nudged the material off one breast.

"Not what you had in mind?" His tongue circled her tight nipple.

"It's exactly what I want." She arched her back, her fingers tightening convulsively. "I feel…"

"Tell me," he urged, eager to hear what effect his mouth was having on her body. He flicked his tongue across her nipple. She jerked in surprise. "I want to know everything. What do you like? What drives you wild?"

At last she unclenched her fingers and spread the shirt wide. Now it was Nic's turn to suck in his breath. She was beautiful. Breathtaking. Perfect. Her small round breasts, topped with dark pink nipples, were a perfect fit in his palm. Pity his mouth would be the only part of him to enjoy all that silky skin. And yet, as he pulled one bud into his mouth and sucked, perhaps that wasn't so bad after all.

She was mewling with gratifying abandon by the time he finished with one breast and moved to the other.

The situation was swiftly disintegrating. Nic felt his control slipping. Heaving a sigh, he caught the edges of her shirt and pulled them together, hiding her gorgeous breasts from his greedy eyes.

"You're stopping?" She sounded appalled. "But things were just starting to get interesting."

His muscles clenched at her frustrated wail. He levered himself out of bed and kept his eyes averted from her. He'd survived temptation once. He wasn't sure he could do it twice.

"You still don't get it, do you? I can't offer you anything beyond this bed."

"I know."

She rolled onto her side, her gaze steady on him. Accusations darted like deer through her gray-green eyes. Anger surged in his chest. Damn her for coming here and littering the clear path to his future with enticement and regret. He retreated to the bathroom. Just before closing the door, he shot a last glance in her direction. She had propped her head on her hand and lay watching him through half-closed lids.

She'd left the edges of her shirt unfastened and the three-inch gap gave him an eye-popping view of the curve of her right breast, almost to the nipple. Aphrodite in all her glory could not have appealed to him more than Brooke's slim form in his bed.

Nic shut the bathroom door with more force than necessary and started the shower. A cold shower, he decided.

As she heard the water start, Brooke exhaled raggedly and rolled onto her back. The empty bed mocked her. Frustration bubbled in her chest and rose into her throat, building into a shriek. She clamped her teeth to prevent any sound from escaping, but it was an effort to hold so much emotion in. So she grabbed one of Nic's pillows and covered her face in it to prevent him from hearing her shrill curses.

Once the tantrum had passed, she lay with her nose buried in the cool cotton, absorbing Nic's scent and reliving the moment when his control had broken. Heat wafted off her skin in surging waves, the source the smoking hot place between her thighs that pulsed and throbbed with frustrated longing. The man had a gift for turning her world upside down.

He only had to give her the slightest bit of encouragement and she went all in. How many times since she'd first discovered she had feelings for him had he crushed her hopes by deflecting her overtures or chasing her away when she'd tried to get him to take a break from a problem so he could gain some perspective on it?

Not for the first time an ache built in her chest. What had started out as a whim, a crush, a foolish game had escalated into something she couldn't break free from.

Her mother, Theresa, even Glen, had warned her she was better off with a man who appreciated her. But she hadn't wanted to hear the good advice from her friends and family. And for a while things had been perfect.

The way she'd felt about him the first time he'd kissed her six months ago was nothing compared to the growing connection she felt now. Each day in his presence it grew stronger. How was she supposed to just let him go and move forward? To raise this child on her own? To spend the rest of her life without him? Panic assailed her, causing dark spots in her vision and making it hard to draw a full breath for several minutes.

She rode the paralyzing fear until her emotions calmed. Able to think rationally again, Brooke was mortified by how badly she wanted to cling to Nic and beg him to give up his responsibilities and be with her. Once upon a time she'd prided herself on being an independent woman, capable of living abroad for a year in Italy while she worked on her doctoral thesis on Italian literature. She might make decisions based on emotion rather than logic, but she ruled her finances with a miser's tight fist and had a knack for avoiding bad relationships.

These days she was a rickety ladder of vulnerability and loose screws. What else could explain why she'd charged a fifteen-hundred-dollar airplane ticket on her credit card to chase after a man who'd vanished from her life without even a goodbye? If she'd picked up the phone and delivered her news about the pregnancy she could have saved herself a bucketful of heartache and said to hell with closure.

Brooke sat up and buttoned Nic's shirt once more. A sudden bout of nausea caught her off guard. If the positive pregnancy test result had seemed surreal, here was tangible proof that her body was irrevocably changed. Brooke slipped off the bed and fled the room, afraid Nic would exit the bathroom and catch her looking green and out of sorts, then demand to know what was wrong with her.

On her way to the guesthouse, she snagged a bit of bread and a bottle of water. Once there, she nibbled at the crust, put the chilled bottle to her warm forehead and willed her stomach to settle down. As the nausea subsided, Brooke's confidence ebbed away, as well.

In twenty-four hours Nic was heading home to find a wife. He would be forever lost to her. Maybe she should give up this madness today and run back to California.

Because she still hadn't done what she'd come here to do: tell Nic she was pregnant.

And yet, on the heels of all she'd learned, did it make sense to burden him with the news that his illegitimate child would be living far from him in California? He was returning home to find a bride and start a family. His future wife wouldn't be happy to find out Nic had already gotten another woman pregnant.

Then, too, he'd proved himself an honorable man. It would tear him apart to know he wouldn't be a part of his child's life? What if he demanded partial custody? Was she going to spend the next eighteen years shuffling their child across the Atlantic Ocean so that he or she could know Nic? And what about the scandal this would mean for the royal family? Maybe in America no one thought twice when celebrities had children without being married, but that wouldn't sit well where European nobility were concerned.

Yet morally was it right to keep the information from him? It would certainly be easier on her. Nic had turned his back on Glen and their dream of getting *Griffin* off the ground. Brooke knew she could count on her brother to keep her secret. Her life going forward would be quiet and routine. She would teach at Berkeley or UCLA and throw herself into raising her child. No one would ever know that she'd had a brief affair with a European prince.

Both options had their positives and negatives. And it was early in her pregnancy. So many things could go wrong in the first trimester. She could take another month to decide. The discovery that she was pregnant was only a week old. Maybe if she gave the situation some more thought she could arrive at a decision that she could live with.

Knowing that avoiding a decision was not the best answer, she dressed in black shorts and a white T-shirt. Maybe she would take a hike to the windmills a little later. Although her stomach wasn't back to normal, she had to act as if nothing was wrong.

Half an hour after her encounter with Nic, she returned to the house and found him standing in the kitchen drinking coffee. He was staring out the window as Brooke drew near and when she saw the expression on his face, all the energy drained from her body.

"Don't." Her throat contracted before she could finish.

He swiveled his head in her direction. His gaze was hollow. "Don't what?"

Hearing his tight, unhappy tone, frustration replaced anxiety. Brooke stamped her foot. "Don't regret what just happened."

"Brooke, you don't understand—"

"Don't," she interrupted, despair clutching at her chest. She didn't need to be psychic to know what ran through Nic's mind. "Don't you dare spew platitudes at me. I've known you too long."

"You don't know me at all."

And whose fault was that? She sucked in a breath. Harsh words gathered in her head. She squeezed her eyes shut, moderated her tone. "I wish we had time to change that."

The umber eyes that turned in her direction were a

stark landscape of cynicism and regret. "But we don't." Although he pushed her away with his words, the muscle jumping in his jaw proclaimed he wasn't happy to do so. His agonized expression matched the pain throbbing in his voice. "My family needs me."

I need you. Your child needs you.

But all of a sudden she knew she wasn't going to put that burden on him. What he felt for her wasn't casual. She was finding it hard to let go. He was going through something similar. But they each had their ways of coping and she should respect that.

Brooke retreated to the opposite side of the room and picked up her sandals. The silence in the house went unbroken for several moments while she reorganized her emotions and set aside her disappointment.

"Are these okay for a hike up to the windmills?" she asked, indicating the footwear. "I'm afraid I don't have anything more sturdy."

"They should be fine." He assessed her feet. "There's a well-defined path up to get there."

"Great."

His brow creased at her flat tone. "Are you okay?"

"Fine. Just feeling a little off all of a sudden. Nothing breakfast won't cure."

Brooke was glad that Elena picked that moment to enter the house with bags of groceries. It kept her and Nic from plunging back into heated waters. With Elena bustling around the kitchen they had little need to exchange more than a few words over a meal of eggs and pastries.

An hour later, they were heading to the windmill. The paved road that led from the town past Nic's villa gave out two miles farther. Ahead was the narrow path cluttered with large rocks and tree roots that led to the three windmills she'd seen on arriving at Ithaca. Nic set a moderate pace through the irregular terrain, forcing Brooke to focus on where she stepped, and silence filled the space between them. For once she was grateful for the lack of conversation because she had too many conflicting thoughts circling her mind.

"There are a number of windmills on Ithaca," Nic began as the brush lining the path ahead of them gave way to a flat, rocky expanse. Brooke was glad for her sunglasses as they emerged from the vegetation onto the rocky plateau.

Before them lay the three disused windmills. Twenty feet in diameter, thirty feet tall, their squat, round shapes stood sentinel over all the boats coming and going from the harbor. Their walls once would have been whitewashed, but years of wind and weather had scoured the brick, returning it to shades of gray and tan.

Nic headed toward the structures, his words drifting back to her on the strong breeze. "Corn and wheat would come from all over the islands to be ground here because of the constant winds in this area."

In the lee of the squat towers, Nic gestured to direct her attention through a curved doorway into the windmill's interior. "As you can see, the 1953 earthquake caused the grinding wheel and shaft to break and tumble to the bottom."

"Fascinating." But her attention was only half on the scene before her. A moment earlier she'd stumbled when her toe caught on a half-buried rock and he'd caught her arm to steady her. His hand had not yet fallen away. "Thank you for bringing me here. The view is amazing. I can see why you enjoy coming to the island."

"After this we should take the boat to Vathay and have lunch." He was obviously hoping that by keeping busy they could avoid a repeat of the morning's events.

Brooke wasn't sure she could spend a fun-filled afternoon with him while her heart was in the process of shattering. For the first time since her interest in him had sparked, she was bereft of hope. Even after he'd broken things off a month ago, she hadn't really believed it was over. This morning, she'd finally faced up to reality.

Nic was going to marry someone else and build a life with that person.

"If you don't mind," Brooke said, "I think I'd rather just hang out on the terrace and do a little reading. But you go ahead and do whatever it is you've been doing before I got here."

He frowned, obviously unsure what to make of her abrupt about-face. "If that's what you want to do."

"It is." The words sounded heavy.

"Very well."

For the next fifteen minutes, he inundated her with facts about the area, the aftereffects of the 1953 earthquake and other interesting tidbits about the island. Brooke responded with nods and polite smiles when he paused to see if she was listening. Eventually, he ran out of things to say and they headed back down the path. They had to walk single file until they reached the road. Once they got there they strode side by side without speaking. When Nic's villa was less than a mile away, to Brooke's surprise, it was Nic who broke the silence.

"About this morning."

"Please don't," Brooke murmured, expelling her breath in a weary sigh.

"I was wrong to kiss you," he continued, either not hearing her protest or ignoring it. "I'm sending you mixed messages and that isn't fair."

"It was my fault. I shouldn't have intruded on your sleep and thrown myself at you. Most men would have taken advantage of the situation. You showed great restraint."

"Nevertheless." His frown indicated he wasn't happy she'd taken the blame. "I haven't been fair to you. If I'd told you from the start who I really was, you'd never have developed feelings for me."

Brooke couldn't believe what she was hearing. She'd chased this man for five years, teased him, flattered him, poured her heart out to him and received nothing in return until six months ago when he'd kissed her. *He'd* kissed *her.* She hadn't plunked herself onto his lap and tormented him the way she'd done the day before. In fact, she hadn't even flirted with him that night. He'd been the one to draw her away from Glen's party and kiss her senseless.

"I never meant to hurt you."

"You haven't." She wasn't upset with him. She was disappointed in herself. How could she have been such a fool for so long? "If I hurt right now it's because I didn't listen when you told me over and over that we weren't right for each other. I created my own troubles. Your conscience should be clear."

She walked faster, needing some space from Nic. He matched her stride for stride.

"Is this some sort of ploy—?"

She erupted in exasperation. "Get over yourself already. I'm done." She gestured broadly with her arms as her temper flared. "You've convinced me that it's stupid to keep holding on for something that can never be. So, congratulations, I'm never going to ask you for anything ever again."

Her anger wasn't reasonable, but at that moment it was the only way to cope with her deep sadness. She couldn't cry, not yet, so she took refuge in ferocity. This was a side of her she'd never let Nic see. She always kept things light and fun around him. Even when she showed him her temper, it was followed by a quicksilver smile.

Right now she had no lightness inside her, only shadow.

Nic caught her arm to slow her as she surged forward. "I don't want us to end like this."

She was not going to say nice things so he could ease his

conscience about her. "End like what? Me being upset with you? How do you think I felt a month ago when you told me that sleeping together had been the wrong thing to do?"

"I was wrong not to tell you the truth about what was really going on." The intense light in his eyes seared through her defenses. "I'm sorry."

Unbidden, sympathy rose in her. Brooke cast it aside. She didn't want to accept that he was as much a victim of circumstances as she. With a vigorous shake of her head she pulled free and began walking once again.

"What happened isn't fair to either one of us," he called after her. "Don't you think if I could choose you I would?"

She swung around and walked backward as she spoke. "The trouble is, you didn't choose me. Nothing is really forcing you to go home and make this huge sacrifice for your country. This is your decision. You feel honor bound. It's who you are. It's why I love you. But don't blame circumstances or your family's expectations for the choice you are making."

Leaving him standing in the middle of the road, Brooke ran the rest of the way back to the villa.

Six

Nic lay on his back, forearm thrown over his eyes. Moonlight streamed into his room like a searchlight, but he couldn't be bothered to close the shutters. A soft breeze trailed across his bare chest, teasing him with the memory of Brooke's fingers tantalizing his skin this morning.

The regret he'd been trying unsuccessfully to contain for the past twelve hours pounded him as relentlessly as the Ionian Sea against the cliff below the villa. Any sensible man would have taken Brooke to bed rather than inflict on her a long sightseeing adventure to busted-up windmills. Instead he'd rejected her not once but twice this morning, and then disregarded the pain he'd caused.

She'd eaten lunch by herself on the terrace and barely spoken to him during dinner. When she did speak, her tone had been stiff. He didn't blame her for being upset. Any apology he might make would've been way too little and far too late. But he'd been relieved when she'd escaped as soon as the dishes had been piled in the sink.

He gusted out an impatient breath and sat up. Sleeping without the benefit of too much alcohol had been hard enough before Brooke arrived. Knowing she slept thirty feet away made unconsciousness completely impossible. Hell. It used to be that if he couldn't sleep, he would work. That outlet was lost to him now. Still, he hadn't yet looked at the forty emails restored to his inbox. Maybe a few hours of technical questions would take his mind off his problems.

Padding barefoot downstairs, he stopped short as he neared the bottom, his skin tingling in awareness that he wasn't alone.

Beyond the open French doors, the full moon slanted a stripe of ethereal white across the harbor's smooth surface and reached into the living room to touch the couch. Beside the shaft of moonlight, a dark shadow huddled, an ink spot on the pristine fabric.

Brooke.

His breath lodged in his throat and her name came out of him in a hoarse whisper. His body went into full alert. This was bad. Very bad. A late-night encounter with her was more temptation than he was prepared to handle.

"How come you're not in bed?" he demanded, stepping onto the limestone tile. He took two steps toward the couch, his impulses getting the upper hand. He'd come close enough to smell vanilla and hear her unsteady breathing. He set one hand on his hip and rubbed the back of his neck with the other.

"I couldn't sleep." Her voice emerged from shadow, low and passionless with a slight waver. "I haven't been able to stop thinking about what I said to you earlier. You're doing the right thing where your family and country are concerned."

"This whole thing is my fault. You came a long way

not knowing who I was or what my family has been going through."

If circumstances were different...

But it wasn't fair to patronize her with meaningless platitudes. Circumstances were exactly what they were and he'd made his decision based on what he'd been taught to do.

"Still, I shouldn't have hit you with a guilt trip."

"You didn't." Nic took another two steps and stopped. His breath hissed through clenched teeth. What was he doing? The longing to gather her into his arms and comfort her stunned him with its power. His body ached to feel her soft body melt against him. Madness.

"I just wanted you to choose me for once."

Her words slammed into his gut and rocked him backward. He'd been a first-class bastard where she was concerned. How many times had he rebuffed her when all she wanted was to help him work through a problem? So what if her methods sounded illogical and ineffective? She'd been right the time she'd badgered him into playing miniature golf with her when he was busy trying to solve a difficult technical problem. On the fourth hole the solution had popped into his head with no prompting. Had he bothered to thank her before rushing back to his workroom at the hangar and burying himself in the project once more?

And now, it was too late to make everything up to her.

"You should head back to bed. You have a long flight back to California tomorrow."

Her shadow moved as she shook her head. "I'm not going home tomorrow."

"Where are you going?"

"I don't know yet. I have a few weeks before I have to be back at UC Santa Cruz. I thought maybe I'd head to Rome and meet up with some friends."

"What about your Berkeley interview?"

"It's the day after tomorrow."

"But you said it was in a few weeks."

"It was rescheduled."

"Why didn't you tell me?" Annoyance flared, banishing all thoughts of comforting her.

"I thought if you knew, you'd put me on a plane right away and I wanted these two days with you."

Two days during which they'd argued and he'd done nothing but push her away. Irritation welled.

"But why aren't you going right home for the interview? Teaching at Berkeley is all you've talked about since I've known you."

Her temper sparked in response to his scolding. "Plans change. It's just not the right time for me to take the position."

"Are you giving up something as important as Berkeley because of me?"

"Seems foolish, doesn't it?" she countered without a trace of bitterness.

Nic clenched his fists. She was going to be so much better without him.

And he was going to be so much worse.

"You should take your own advice about going to bed," she told him. "Sounds like your mother planned a grueling week for you. It will be better if you're well rested."

Nic had the distinct impression he'd just been dismissed. His lips twitched. He could always count on Brooke to do the last thing he expected. After her assault on his willpower this morning, he'd been lying awake half expecting her to launch another all-out attack tonight.

From the way he'd been with her this morning, she had to know he was having a harder and harder time resisting her. Resisting what he wanted more than anything. With each beat of his heart, the idea of taking her back upstairs and tumbling her into his bed seemed less like a huge mistake and more like the right thing to do.

Walk away.

"What are you going to do?" he asked, knowing that prolonging this conversation was the height of idiocy. It would only make going back to bed alone that much harder.

"Sit here."

"I won't be able to sleep knowing you're down here in the dark."

A small smile filled her voice as she said, "You've never had trouble putting me out of your mind before."

If she only knew. "You weren't sitting on my couch in your pajamas before."

Her sigh was barely audible over the blood thundering in his ears.

"Good night." Calling himself every sort of fool, he headed back upstairs. Leaving his bedroom door open in a halfhearted invitation, he fell onto the mattress. Hands behind his head, eyes on the ceiling, he strained to hear footfalls on the stairs. The house was completely silent except for the breeze stirring the curtains on either side of his window.

His nerves stretched and twisted, but she didn't appear. He caught himself glancing at the doorway, expecting her silhouette. As the minutes ticked by, Nic forced his eyes shut, but he couldn't quiet his mind and the past two days played through his thoughts with unrelenting starkness.

With a heated curse, he rolled off the bed and stalked downstairs. It didn't surprise him to find her exactly where he'd left her.

"You are the most stubborn woman I've ever known," he complained. "I don't know what the hell you expect from me."

Even his mother had given up trying to keep him in Sherdana when his heart belonged in an airplane hangar in the Mojave Desert. But for years Brooke had relent-lessly pushed herself into his life until he couldn't celebrate achievements or face failures without thinking about her.

"My expectations are all in the past," she said, push-ing to her feet.

And that's what was eating him alive.

They stared at each other in motionless silence until Brooke heaved a huge sigh. The dramatic rise and fall of her chest snagged Nic's attention. The tank top she wore scooped low in front, offering him the tiniest hint of cleav-age. Recalling the way her breasts had tasted this morn-ing, he repressed a groan.

"Brooke."

"Don't." She started past him. Nic caught her wrist. At his touch, she stilled. "I thought I was pretty clear this af-ternoon when I said that I've given up on you."

"Crystal clear." Nic cupped her face, his fingers sliding into the silky strands of russet near her ear.

"Then what are you doing?"

"Wishing you didn't have to."

He brought his mouth down to hers, catching her lips in a searing kiss that held nothing back. She stiffened, her body bracing to recoil. He couldn't let that happen. Not now. Not when he'd stopped being principled and noble. Not when he wanted her with a hunger that ate at him like acid.

Taking a tighter grip on her wrist, he slowly levered it behind her back, compelling her hips forward until her pelvis brushed against the jut of his erection. The con-tact made him moan. He deepened the kiss, sweeping his tongue forward to taste her. Her lips parted for him. A soft whimper escaped her throat as she writhed in his grasp, but whether she fought to escape or move closer he couldn't be sure.

"I want you," he murmured, setting his mouth on her throat and sucking gently.

Her body trembled, but her muscles remained tense. Labored, uneven breaths pushed her breasts against his bare chest.

"Damn you, Nic." It was in her voice, in the way she tilted her head to allow him better access to her neck. She was furious and aroused. "It's too late for you to change your mind."

"It's too late when I say it is." He released her wrist and cupped her small, round butt in his palm. The cotton pajama bottoms bunched as he gave a light squeeze.

She gasped, set both hands on his chest and shoved. It was like a kitten batting at a mastiff. "This isn't fair."

"Fair?" He growled the word. "Do you want to talk about fair? You've tormented me for five years. Strutting around the hangar in your barely there denim shorts. Coming to peer over my shoulder and letting your hair tickle my skin. How hard do you think it was for me to keep from pulling you into my lap and putting my hands all over you?"

"You never..." She arched back and stared up into his face. "I had no idea."

"I made sure you didn't. But it wasn't easy." He wrapped his fingers around her red curls and gave a gentle but firm tug. "And it wasn't fun."

Brooke was electrified by Nic's admission; the twinge in her scalp when he pulled her hair merely enhanced her already overstimulated nerves. She welcomed the discomfort. The fleeting pain chased the last vestiges of self-pity from her mind and grounded her in the moment.

Taking her silence and stillness as surrender, Nic bent to kiss her again, but Brooke turned aside at the last minute. Even though this was what she'd wanted when bought her plane ticket, she wasn't the same woman who'd gotten on the plane in San Francisco.

Nic wasn't deterred by her evasion. He kissed his way across her cheek and seized her earlobe between his teeth. Her knees wavered as his unsteady breath filled her ear. Meanwhile, his hands moved over her back, gliding beneath her tank top to find her hot skin and trace each bump of her spine.

"What's wrong?" he murmured as his lips investigated the hollow made by her collarbone.

"You want me to give in." He was doing whatever it took to make her putty in his hand. "Just like you used to want me to leave you alone. It's always about what you want."

She felt as much as heard his sigh. His hands left her body and bracketed his hips. He regarded her solemnly.

"I thought this was what we both wanted."

A breeze puffed in from the terrace, chilling Brooke. Where a second earlier the room had been dark, moonlight now poured over the tiled floor and bathed Nic's splendid torso in a white glow. Her mouth went dry as her gaze traced the rise and fall of his pecs and abs, the perfect ratio of broad shoulders to narrow hips. Although still in shadow, the planes of his face seemed more chiseled, his jaw sharper.

Her pulse began to slam harder, throbbing in her wrist, her throat and between her thighs. She found his eyes in the dimness, fell beneath the hypnotic power of his gaze. A rushing filled her ears, the incessant movement of a stream as it surges past boulders and fallen trees, unstoppable. Once upon a time, she'd been like that, full of purpose and joy. Then she'd let her doubts bottle her up.

Was she really going to stand here being annoyed with him and waste another second of the limited time she had left bemoaning the cards fate had dealt?

She held out her hand to Nic. He linked his fingers with hers and drew her toward the stairs. Without saying a word they entered his bedroom and came together in a slow, effortless dance of hands, lips and tongue. Pajamas landed on the floor and Brooke stretched out on Nic's king-size bed, his strong body pressing her hard into the mattress as they kissed and explored.

Words were lost to Brooke as Nic's fingertips rode her rib cage to the undersides of her breasts. She couldn't remember ever feeling so heavy and so light at the same time. Arching her spine, she pushed her nipples against his palms. Stars burst behind her eyelids as he circled the hard buds, making them ache with pleasure before at long last drawing one, then the other, into his hot mouth.

The sensations snapping along her nerves made Brooke quiver and gasp. She was hungry for Nic to touch her more intimately, but her senses had gone fuzzy, her body languid. His hand rode upward along her inner thigh with torturous precision and she followed its progress with breaths growing ever more faint. By the time his finger dipped into her wet heat, her lungs had forgotten how to function. She lay with her eyes closed, her head spinning as he filled her first with one, then two fingers, stretching her, finding the spot that caused her hips to jerk and the first shuddering moan to escape her throat.

And then he replaced his hand with his mouth and adored her with tongue and teeth. Sliding his hands beneath her butt, he lifted her against the press and retreat of his kiss. She tried to squirm, to escape the tongue that drove her relentlessly toward pleasure so acute it hurt, but Nic dug his fingers into her skin and held her captive. Mewling, Brooke surrendered to the slow, tantalizing rise of ecstasy.

Nic hadn't made love to her like this the first time they were together. Five years of anticipation had made their lovemaking passionate and impatient. Nic had satisfied her three times that night, his large body surging into hers, filling her completely. She'd come with desperate cries, unable to articulate the incandescent heights to which he'd lifted her.

But the rush upward had been followed by only a brief respite to catch her breath and savor the afterglow. Nic had proved insatiable that night and when at last they'd spent the last of their passion, she'd fallen into a deep, dreamless slumber.

This was different. As if recognizing this was their last time together, he made love to her with his eyes first and then his hands. Languid sweeps of his lips across her skin soothed her soul and set her skin aflame. Words of appreciation and praise poured over her while his fingers reverently grazed the lines of her body.

By the time he slipped on a condom and settled between her thighs, Brooke wasn't sure where she ended and he began. He moved slowly into her, easing in just the head of his erection, giving her time she didn't need to adjust to him.

Tipping her hips as he began his second thrust, she ensured that his forward progress didn't end until he was fully seated inside her. He groaned and buried his face in her neck. She dug her fingernails into his back, reveling in the fullness of his possession. For a long moment neither of them moved. Brooke filled her lungs with the spicy tang of his aftershave and the musk of their lovemaking. She closed her eyes to memorize the feel of his powerful body as he began moving.

Measured and deliberate, Nic rocked against her, thrusting in and out while pleasure built. He kissed her hard, his tongue plunging to tangle with hers. Their hips came together with increased urgency. Brooke let her teeth glide along Nic's neck. He bucked hard against her when she nipped at his skin. The thrust rapped her womb where their child grew and sent her spiraling toward climax. She must have clenched around him because suddenly Nic picked up the pace. Together they climbed, hands pleasuring, bodies striving for closeness. Brooke came first, Nic's name on her lips. He drove into her more urgently and reached orgasm moments later.

His strong body shook with the intensity of his release and a hoarse cry spilled out of him. What followed was the deepest, most emotionally charged kiss he'd ever given her. Brooke clung to him while her body pulsed with aftershocks and surrendered to the tempest raging in Nic. If she'd thought their lovemaking had forever branded her as his, the kiss, tender one moment, joyous the next, stole the heart right out of her body.

"Incredible." He buried his face in her neck, his breath heavy and uneven, body limp and powerless.

Brooke wrapped her arms around his shoulders, marveling that this formidable man had been reduced to overcooked noodles in her arms. Grinning, she stroked the bumpy length of his spine and ran her nails through his hair in a soothing caress.

"Am I too heavy?" he murmured, lips moving against her shoulder as he spoke.

"A little, but I don't want you to move just yet." She was afraid any shift would disrupt this moment of perfect harmony.

"Good. I like it just where I am."

They stayed that way for a long time. Legs entwined, his breath soft and steady on her neck, his fingers playing idly in her tangled curls. Brooke couldn't recall if she'd ever enjoyed being so utterly still before. She didn't want to talk or to think. Only to be.

But as with all things, change is inevitable. Nic heaved a mighty sigh and rolled away from her to dispose of the condom and pull a sheet over their cooling bodies. The breeze had shifted direction and the air that had seemed dense and sultry an hour earlier was swept away.

With her head pillowed on his shoulder and Nic's fingers absently gliding across the small of her back, the lethargy she'd experienced earlier didn't return.

"I can feel you thinking," Nic said, his eyes closed, a half smile curving his lips.

"That's illogical."

His chest moved up and down with his sigh. "If I was in a logical frame of mind, I wouldn't be lying naked with you in my arms."

"I suppose not."

"What's on your mind?"

Not wanting to share her true thoughts, she said the first thing that popped into her head. "If you must know I was thinking about getting a cat when I get home."

"Really?" He sounded genuinely surprised. "I thought Glen said you guys grew up with dogs."

"We did, but dogs are so needy and some of my days can go really long with classes and office hours. I think a cat would be a wiser choice."

"I like cats."

"You do?" She couldn't imagine Nic owning anything that needed regular feeding or care. "Wouldn't a snake be a more suitable pet for you?"

"A snake?"

"Sure, something you only had to feed once a week." She chuckled when he growled at her.

"No snakes." He yawned. "A cat. Definitely."

Brooke could tell by the sleepiness of his voice that she was losing him. "But a cat is going to jump on your worktable and knock things off. It's going to wake you in the middle of the night wanting to be petted and yowling at you for attention. They ignore you when you give them commands and never come when they're called."

Nic cracked open one eye and smirked at her. "Yeah, a cat. They're definitely my favorite kind of nuisance."

It took Brooke a couple seconds to realize he had connected her behavior to what she'd just said about cats. In retaliation, she poked him hard in the ribs and he located the ticklish spot behind her knees that had her squirming. It didn't take long for their good-natured tussling to spark another round of lovemaking.

Much later, while Nic's breathing deepened into sleep, Brooke lay awake in the predawn stillness and tried to keep her thoughts from rushing into the future. The hours she had with him grew shorter every second. So instead of sleeping, as the sky grew lighter, Brooke lost herself in Nic's snug embrace, savored the way his warmth seeped through her skin and awaited the day.

The nausea that had plagued her the day before began as the sun peeked over the horizon and gilded the window ledge. She breathed through the first wave and sagged with relief when her stomach settled down. Remembering how the previous morning had gone, Brooke knew she had to get back to her room. Nic might not be the most observant of men, but even he'd be hard-pressed not to notice if she was throwing up in his bathroom.

Last night while in the grip of insomnia, she'd decided not to tell him she was pregnant. If he hadn't made love to her with such all-consuming emotion, she might have accepted that they could go back to being friends, affectionate but disconnected by distance and circumstances. But now she realized that they had to make a clean break of it. It would be best for both of them if he didn't know the truth.

Before her stomach began to pitch and roll again, Brooke untangled herself from Nic's embrace and eased from his bed. Her head spun sickeningly as she got to her feet and snatched up her pajamas. Naked, the soft cotton pressed to her mouth, she raced from the room and down the stairs.

If Elena was shocked to see her streak by, Brooke never knew because her focus was fixed on crossing the twenty feet of terrace to the guesthouse and reaching the bathroom in the nick of time. Panting in the aftermath, she splashed cold water on her face and waited to see if the nausea had passed. When it appeared the worst was over, Brooke climbed into the shower.

She was dressed and repacking her suitcase when a soft knock sounded. Heart jumping, she eased the door open, expecting to see Nic standing there, and was surprised to see Elena bearing a tray with a teapot and a plate of bread and assorted preserves.

"Ginger tea is good for nausea," she announced, slipping the tray onto the dresser. "I understand you are leaving for Sherdana today."

"Nic is going. I'm heading for Italy." But her plan to visit friends in Rome had lost its appeal. More than anything she wanted to head home to family and friends and start the process of healing in their comforting embrace.

Elena's eyes narrowed. "You let me know if you need anything before you leave."

Seven

Awaking to an empty bed hadn't been the best start to Nic's day, but he reasoned he might as well get used to disappointment because he wouldn't ever wake to Brooke's smile again. The sun was high by the time Nic finished his shower and headed to the first floor. Elena was dusting the already immaculate furniture. She shot him an intensely unhappy look as he poured himself a cup of coffee and he wondered at her barely veiled hostility.

"Have you seen Brooke this morning?" he asked, carrying his cup to the terrace doorway and peering in the direction of the guesthouse. The trip to Kefalonia's airport would take forty-five minutes by boat and another hour over land. They would need to leave soon.

"She has eaten breakfast and had some last minute packing to do."

"Is Thasos ready with the boat?"

Elena nodded. "She is a nice girl. You shouldn't let her go to Italy by herself."

"She is going to visit friends," he explained to the housekeeper, while guilt nibbled at the edges of his conscience. "She knows her way around. She lived in Rome and Florence for a year."

"You should take her home."

Nic was startled by Elena's remark. He'd been thinking the same thing all morning. Unfortunately that wasn't possible. Reality dictated he should distance himself from Brooke as soon as possible, but the thought of letting her go off by herself disturbed him.

If she didn't get on a plane bound for California, he would spend the next two weeks worrying about her traveling alone in Europe instead of focusing on the issues at home and the necessity of finding a wife. Nor did he have time to escort her to the gate and satisfy himself that she was heading to San Francisco. He was expected back in Sherdana this afternoon.

Nic's chest tightened. He was doing a terrible job of lying to himself. In truth he wasn't ready to say goodbye. It was selfish and stupid.

"I need to make a phone call," Nic told Elena. "Will you let Brooke know we'll be leaving in ten minutes?"

Calling himself every sort of idiot, Nic dialed Gabriel. When he answered, Nic got right to the point. "I'm bringing someone home with me. She's come a long way to see me and I don't feel right leaving her alone in Greece."

"She?" Gabriel echoed, not quite able to keep curiosity out of his voice. "Is this going to cause problems?"

Nic knew exactly what Gabriel meant and decided not to sugarcoat it. "That's not my intention. She's Glen's sister. I think I've mentioned her a few times."

"The one who drives you crazy?" Gabriel sounded intrigued.

"The interfering one who flew here to convince me to come back to the *Griffin* project."

"Just the project?"

"What's that supposed to mean?" Nic didn't intend to be defensive, but with last night's events still reverberating across his emotions, he wasn't in the best shape to fence with a diplomat as savvy as Gabriel. "She's Glen's little sister."

"And you talk about her more than any woman you've ever known."

"I know what you're getting at, but it's not an issue. Things got a little complicated between us recently, but everything is sorted out."

"Complicated how?"

"I didn't tell her who I was until she came here looking for me and that upset her. I shouldn't have left her in the dark. We've been…friends…for a long time."

"Why didn't you tell her?"

Nic rubbed his temples where an ache had begun. "I know this is going to be hard for you to understand but I liked being an ordinary scientist, anonymously doing the work I'm really good at."

"You're right. I don't understand. I grew up knowing I belonged to the country. You never did like being in the spotlight. So you didn't tell her you're a prince. Do you think she would have looked at you differently if she'd known all along?"

"Brooke values a person for how they behave not who they are or what they have."

Gabriel laughed. "She sounds like your sort of girl. I can't wait to meet her."

"Honestly, it's not like that." He didn't want his brother giving the wrong idea to their parents. "She understands my situation."

"She knows that you're coming home to find a bride? And she wants to accompany you, anyway?"

"I haven't spoken with her this morning." Not exactly a

lie. "She doesn't know I'm bringing her with me to Sherdana yet."

"Well, this should make for an interesting family dinner," Gabriel said. "I'll make sure there's a place set at the table for her beside Mother."

And before Nic could protest that arrangement, Gabriel hung up. Nic debated calling him back, but decided it would only exacerbate his brother's suspicions about Brooke. Playing it cool and calm around his family would be the best way to handle any and all speculation.

Grabbing his bag from his bedroom, Nic made his way toward the steps that Brooke had used to access the terrace two days ago. They led down the steep hillside in a zigzag that ended at a private dock. Brooke had already arrived at the boat and was settled onto the seat opposite the pilot's chair. The smile she offered Nic was bright if a little ragged around the edges.

Thasos started the engine as soon as Nic stepped aboard and quickly untied the mooring ropes. Nic settled into the bench seat at the back of the boat and watched Brooke pretend not to be interested in him. He knew the signs. He'd spent years giving her the impression he was oblivious to her presence. Yet how could he be? She lit up every room she entered. Her personality set the very air to buzzing. Sitting still was probably the hardest thing she did. Yet when her brain engaged, she could get lost in a book or her writing for hours.

They'd shared many companionable afternoons while she was working on her second doctorate. Not surprisingly, she enjoyed sitting cross-legged on the couch in his workroom, tapping away at her computer keyboard or with her nose buried in a book. If he managed to accomplish any work on the weekends she visited, it was a miracle. Most of the time, he'd pretended to be productive while he watched her surreptitiously.

Forty-five minutes after leaving Ithaca, the boat maneuvered into an open space at the Fiskardo quay. A car would be waiting to carry them on the thirty-one-kilometer journey to the airport outside Kefalonia's capital, Argostoli. If traffic was good, they would get there in a little less than an hour.

Thasos carried their bags to the waiting car and with a jaunty wave turned back to the boat. As soon as he'd driven out of sight, Nic turned to Brooke.

"I don't feel comfortable heading home to Sherdana and leaving you on your own."

"Good Lord, Nic." She shot him a dry look. "I'm perfectly capable of taking care of myself."

"I agree. It's just that with everything that has happened in the last few days—"

"Stop right there." All trace of amusement vanished from her tone as she interrupted him. "After everything that's happened…? I am not some delicate flower that has been crushed by disappointment."

"Nevertheless. I'm not going to leave you stranded in Greece. You are coming home with me."

After five years of teasing and cajoling, bullying and begging, Brooke thought she had Nic all figured out. He preferred working in solitude, hated drama and rarely veered from a goal once he'd set his mind to something. But this announcement left her floundering. Had she ever really known him at all?

"What do you mean you're taking me home with you?" The notion thrilled and terrified her.

"Exactly what I said." Nic's jaw was set in uncompromising lines. "You will fly with me to Sherdana and from there I will make sure you get a flight back to California."

The knot in Brooke's stomach didn't ease with his clarification. "I assure you I'm perfectly capable of ge''ing a flight home from Greece." With morning sickness plaguing her, she'd given up the idea of a summer holiday in Italy. She wanted to be surrounded by familiar things and her favorite people. Maybe she'd spend a week in LA visiting her parents.

"Don't make this difficult on yourself."

"Isn't that what I should be saying to you?" Seeing he didn't comprehend her meaning, Brooke clarified. "Have you considered what happens when we land? How fast can you get me on a plane to the States? In the meantime are you planning on leaving me waiting at the airport? Putting me up in a hotel? Or perhaps you think I'd be more comfortable at the palace?"

Expecting her sarcasm to be lost on him the way it usually was, Brooke was stunned by his matter-of-fact retort.

"My brother said he'll make sure the staff sets an extra place for you at dinner next to my mother." Lighthearted mischief lit his eyes as her mouth dropped open.

"I can't have dinner with your family." Her throat clenched around a lump of panic.

"Why not?"

"I have nothing to wear."

"You look perfect to me."

With lids half-closed, his gaze roamed over her body, setting off a chain reaction of longing and need. The July morning had gone from warm to hot as the sun had crested the horizon and Brooke had dressed accordingly in a loose-fitting blue-and-white cotton peasant dress with a thigh-baring hem and a plunging neckline. The look was fine for traveling from one Greek Island to another or catching a short flight to Rome, London or anywhere else she could snag a connection home to California. But to go to Sherdana and be introduced to Nic's family?

"Why are you really bringing me along?"

"Because I'm not ready to let you go." As light as a

feather, he slid his forefinger along her jaw. It fell away when it reached her chin. "Not yet."

But let her go he would. Her skin tingled where he'd touched her. Brooke saw the regret in his eyes and her heart jerked. Heat kindled in her midsection as she recalled what had taken place between them the night before, but desire tangled with anxiety and sadness. How was she supposed to just walk away?

She jammed her balled fists behind her to hide their shaking and estimated she had half an hour to talk him out of his madness. "Have you considered how unhappy your parents are going to be if you show up with some strange girl in tow?"

"You're not a strange girl. You're Glen's sister."

"And how are you going to explain what I was doing on the island with you?"

"I've already contacted Gabriel and briefed him."

Briefed him with the truth or a diplomatic runaround? "You don't think anyone is going to be suspicious about the nature of our relationship?

"Why would they be? I've spoken of you often to my family. They know you're Glen's annoying baby sister whom I've known for the last five years."

Seeing his wicked smile, she relaxed a little. "Okay, maybe we can do this. After all, Glen knows us better than anyone and he has no idea anything changed between us." If they could fool Glen, they could keep his family from guessing the true nature of their relationship.

"He knows."

Brooke shook her head. "Impossible." Her mind raced over every conversation she'd had with her brother in the past month. "He hasn't said a word."

"He had plenty to say to me," Nic replied in a tight voice, and Brooke suddenly had no trouble imagining how that conversation had gone.

Glen was the best older brother a girl could have. Born eighteen months before her, he'd never minded when she'd tagged after him and his buddies. The guys had accepted her as one of them and taught her how to surf and water-ski. She'd grown up half tomboy, half girlie-girl. They'd all had a great time until Glen graduated high school two years early and headed off to MIT where he'd met Nic.

"The morning after we were together," Nic continued, "your brother cornered me in the lab and threatened to send me up strapped to the rocket if I hurt you."

"No wonder you got out of town so fast after breaking things off with me." Her words were meant to be funny, but when Nic grimaced, she realized her insensitivity. He'd actually left not long after the rocket blew up. "I'm sorry." She looked down at her hands. "I shouldn't have said that."

Nic set his fingers beneath her chin and adjusted the angle of her head until their eyes met. "I'd like to show you my country."

And then what? She received the royal treatment and another goodbye? Already her heart was behaving rashly. She'd opened herself to heartache when she'd surrendered to one last night in his arms. To linger meant parting from him would be that much harder. Did she have no self-control? No self-respect? Hadn't she already learned several difficult lessons?

The need in his gaze echoed the longing in her heart. "Sure," she murmured, surrendering to what they both wanted. "Why not."

"Then that's settled."

An hour later, Nic led her onto a luxurious private plane and guided her into a comfortable leather seat beside the window. With his warm, solid presence bolstering her confidence, Brooke buckled her seat belt and listened to the jet's engine rev. As the plane began to taxi, her chest compressed. Try as she might, she couldn't shake the notion that she should have refused Nic's invitation and just gone home to California.

The instant he'd set foot on the plane his demeanor had changed. Tension rode his broad shoulders and he seemed more distant than ever, his bearing more formal, his expression set into aloof lines. Before leaving Ithaca he'd donned a pair of light beige dress pants and a pale blue dress shirt that set off his tanned skin. On the seat opposite him, he'd placed a beige blazer that bore a blue pocket square. Brooke stared at the oddity.

Nic in stylish clothes. And a coordinating pocket square.

He'd always been sexy, handsome and confident, but he now wore a mantle of überwealthy, ultrasophistication. Ensconced in the luxurious plane, his big hands linked loosely in his lap, he looked utterly confident, poised and…regal. For the first time she truly accepted that Nic was no longer the rocket scientist she knew. Nor was he the ardent lover of last night. Swallowed by helplessness, Brooke stared straight ahead unsure who he'd become.

Maybe leaving him behind in Sherdana was going to be easier than she realized. This Nic wasn't the man she'd fallen in love with. A shiver raced up her spine as his hand covered hers and squeezed gently. Obviously, her heart had no problem with the changes in Nic's appearance. Her pulse fluttered and skipped along just as foolishly as ever.

"Are you okay?" he asked.

Did she explain how his transformation bothered her? To what end? He could never be hers. He belonged to a nation.

"This is quite a plane." Feeling out of place sitting beside such an aristocratic dreamboat on his multimillion-dollar aircraft, Brooke babbled the first thought that entered her head. "Is it yours?"

"If by 'yours' you are asking if it belongs to Sherdana's royal family, then yes."

"Well, that's pretty convenient for you, I guess." She mustered a wry grin. "I suppose the press knows the plane pretty well and that your arrival won't exactly be a state secret."

"Your point?"

"Aside from the fact that we're trying to maintain a low profile on our whole relationship thing, I'm dressed like someone's poor relation. The press is bound to be curious about me. Please can I stay on the plane after you get off until the coast is clear?"

He looked ready to protest, but shook his head and sighed. "If you wish. I'll arrange for someone to meet you at the hangar. That way there won't be any press asking questions you don't want to answer."

It hit Brooke what some of those questions might be and her brain grew sluggish. She'd spent most of her life with her nose buried in books. Glen was the sibling who relished the spotlight. He didn't freeze up in front of large crowds, but put people at ease with his charismatic charm and dazzled them with his intelligence. Numerous times she'd stood back during press events and marveled at his confidence. Not even the difficult questions fired at him after the rocket blew up had rattled him. He'd demonstrated the perfect blend of sadness and determination.

"As for clothes," Nic continued, "I'm sure either my sister, Ariana, or Olivia, Gabriel's wife, will be able to lend you some things."

Brooke would be borrowing clothes from princesses. This wasn't an ordinary family he was taking her home to meet. His mother was a queen. His father was a king. Nic was a prince. What the hell was she doing? She clutched at the armrests, suddenly unable to breathe.

The whirr and clunk of landing gear being locked into place startled her. They were minutes from landing. Nothing about this trip was working out the way she'd planned.

She'd stepped onto the plane in San Francisco thinking she would fly to Greece, tell him about the baby and bring Nic back with her so they could be one big happy family.

The full impact of her foolishness now hit her like a mace. Even if Nic were madly in love with her, he couldn't offer her anything permanent. In fact, he was so far out of her league that they could be living on separate planets.

"I need to know details about your family so I'm prepared," she blurted out, her stomach flipping as the plane lost altitude.

"Sure. Where would you like to start?"

So many questions whirled in her mind that it took her a moment to prioritize them. "Your parents. How do I address them?"

Eight

Nic emerged from the plane and hesitated before descending the stairs to the tarmac. In a tight knot, thirty feet away, a dozen reporters held up cameras and microphones all focused on him. He approached the assembled crowd—the prodigal son returning to the bosom of his family—and answered several questions before heading toward the black Mercedes that awaited him.

Although he'd known it was the sensible thing to do, separating from Brooke even for a short period of time didn't feel right. It wasn't as if he expected her to run off and hop a plane back to California. Enough security surrounded the royal aircraft hangar that she wouldn't get five feet from the plane before she was stopped and questioned.

No, it was more the sense that by traveling separately to the palace, he was acknowledging that there was something to hide. And yet, wasn't there? During the car ride to the airport when she'd asked him why he wanted her to come home with him, he'd told her the truth. He wasn't ready to let her go. The answer had distressed her.

Last night she'd accused him of always demanding things be his way. Now, once again he was acting selfishly.

Nic passed the crowd of reporters without another glance. A familiar figure stood beside the car's rear door. Stewart Barnes, Gabriel's private secretary, offered a smile and a nod as Nic approached.

"Good afternoon, Your Highness. I hope you had a good flight from Greece." The secretary's keen blue eyes darted toward the plane. "Prince Gabriel mentioned you were bringing someone with you. Did she change her mind?"

"No. She's just a little skittish about public appearances. Could you arrange a car to pick her up at the hangar?"

If Stewart was surprised that Nic was sneaking a girl into the country, his expression didn't show it. "Of course." He bowed and opened the car door.

Because the car windows were tinted, Nic had no idea anyone besides the driver was in the vehicle. Therefore, when he spotted Gabriel sitting in the backseat and grinning at him, Nic was overcome by an unexpected rush of joy.

"Good heavens, what are you doing here?" Nic embraced his brother as Stewart closed the door, encasing the princes in privacy.

"It's been three years since you've come home and you have to ask? I've missed you."

The genuine thrum of affection in Gabriel's voice caught Nic off guard. As tight as the triplets had been as children, once on their divergent paths, circumstances and distance had caused them to drift apart. Nic hadn't realized how much he'd missed his older brother until this moment.

"I've missed you, too." The car began to move as Nic asked after the youngest of the three brothers. "How's Christian?"

"Unpredictable as always. Right now he's in Switzerland talking to a company that might be interested in bringing a nanotechnology manufacturing plant here."

"That's wonderful." Nic couldn't help but wonder at the timing of Christian's absence given the series of events his mother had designed for the purpose of finding brides for her sons. "When is he due back?"

"In time for the wedding or Mother will skin him alive."

"And the rest of the parties and receptions?"

Gabriel laughed. "All eyes will be on you."

Nic marveled at the change in his earnest brother. Although young Gabriel had been as full of curiosity and mischief as Nic and Christian, somewhere around his tenth birthday it had hit him that the leadership of the country would one day be his. Almost overnight, while his inquisitive nature had remained, he'd become overly serious and all too responsible.

"You're different," Nic observed. "I don't remember the last time you were this…"

"Happy?" Gabriel's eyes glinted. "It's called wedded bliss. You should try it."

A woman had done this to Gabriel? "I'm looking forward to meeting your wife."

"And speaking of fair women, what happened to your Brooke?"

"She's not my Brooke." Nic heard gravel in his voice and moderated his tone. "And she's staying in the plane until it's taxied into the hangar."

"Your idea or hers?"

"Hers. She was concerned that she wasn't dressed properly and wanted to maintain a low profile."

Gabriel's eyes widened in feigned shock. "What was she wearing that she was so unpresentable?"

"I don't know. Some sort of cotton dress. She thought she looked like someone's poor relation."

"Did she?"

Nic thought she looked carefree and sexy. "Not at all, but what do I know about women's fashion?"

The two men fell to talking about recent events including the incident where the vengeful aunt of Gabriel's twin daughters had infiltrated the palace intending to stop him from marrying Olivia.

"And you have no idea where she's gone?" Nic quizzed, amazed how much chaos one woman had created.

"Interpol has interviewed her former employer and visited her flat in Milan, but for now she's on the run."

As the car entered the palace grounds, Nic's mind circled back to the woman he'd left at the airport. "Have you told anyone besides Stewart that I brought Brooke with me?"

"Olivia and her secretary, Libby, know. They are prepared to take charge of her as soon as she arrives."

"Thank you." Nic was relieved that Brooke would be taken care of.

"Oh, and Mother is expecting you in the blue drawing room for tea. She has an hour blocked out for you to view the first round of potential wives. Stewart interviewed several secretary candidates for you. Their résumés will be waiting in your room. Look them over and let Stewart know which you'd like to meet."

"A secretary?"

"Now that you're back, we've packed your agenda with meetings and appearances. You'll need someone to keep you on schedule."

Nic's head spun. "Damn," he muttered. "It feels as if I never left."

Gabriel clapped him on the shoulder. "It's good to have you back."

From the backseat of a luxurious Mercedes, Brooke clutched her worn travel bag and watched the town of

Carone slip past. In the many years she'd known Nic, which she'd spent alternately being ignored and rejected, she'd never once been as angry with him as she was at this moment.

What had he been thinking to bring her to Sherdana? She didn't belong here. She didn't fit into his world the way he'd fit into hers. No doctorate degrees could prepare her for the pitfalls of palace life. She'd be dining with his family. What fork did she use? She would stand out as the uncouth American accustomed to eating burgers and fries with her fingers. Brooke frowned as she considered how many of her favorite foods didn't require a knife and fork. Pizza. Tacos. Pulled pork sandwiches.

And what if she couldn't get a flight out in the next day or two? As Nic's guest, would she be expected to attend any of the parties his mother had arranged? Were they the sort of parties where people danced? Nic had already shown her a dance specific to the country. They'd laughed over her inability to master the simplest of steps. She'd never imagined a time when she'd be expected to perform them.

And the biggest worry of all: What if someone discovered she was pregnant? Now that morning sickness was hitting her hard, what excuse could she make to explain away the nausea?

Brooke gawked like any tourist as the car swung through a gate and the palace appeared. Nic had grown up here. The chasm between them widened even further. It was one thing to rationalize that her brother's business partner was in reality the prince of a small European country. It was another to see for herself.

During her year abroad in Italy she'd been fortunate enough to be invited to several palaces. A few of the older volumes of Italian literature she'd used in her doctoral thesis had been housed in private collections and she'd been lucky enough to be allowed the opportunity to study them. But those residences had been far less grand and much smaller than the enormous palace she was heading toward right now.

The car followed a circular driveway around a massive fountain and drew up in front of the palace's wide double doors. Surprise held Brooke in place. Given her stealthy transfer from the royal private plane to this car, she'd half expected to be dropped off at the servants' back entrance.

A man in a dark blue suit stepped forward and opened the car door. Brooke stared at the palace doors, unable to make her legs work. One of the tall doors moved, opening enough to let a slim woman in a burgundy suit slip through. Still unsure of her circumstances, Brooke waited as the woman approached.

"Dr. Davis?" She had a lovely soft voice and a British accent. "I'm Libby Marshall, Princess Olivia's private secretary."

"Nice to meet you." Brooke still hadn't budged from the car. "Nic didn't mention he intended to bring me here when we left his villa this morning so I'm not really sure about all this."

The princess's secretary smiled. "Don't worry, all has been arranged. Princess Olivia is looking forward to meeting you. Armando will take your bag. If you will follow me."

If she hadn't flown hundreds of miles in a private jet, Brooke might have been giddy at the thought that a princess was looking forward to meeting her. Instead, it was just one more in a series of surreal experiences.

Brooke slipped from the car and let herself gawk at the sheer size of the palace. Her escort moved like someone who knew better than to keep people waiting and had disappeared through the tall doors by the time Brooke surrendered her meager possessions to Armando. She trotted to catch up, but slowed as soon as she stepped inside.

The palace was everything she'd expected. Thirty feet before her a black-and-white marble floor ended in a wide staircase covered in royal blue carpet. The stairs were wide enough to let an SUV pass. They were split into two sections. The first flight ascended to a landing that then split into separate stairs that continued their climb to the second floor.

She envisioned dozens of women dressed in ball gowns of every color, gliding down that staircase, hands trailing along the polished banister, all coming to meet Nic as he stood, formally dressed, on the polished marble at the bottom of the stairs awaiting them. His gaze would run along the line of women, his expression stern and unyielding as he searched for his perfect bride.

Brooke saw herself bringing up the rear. She was late and the borrowed dress she wore would be too long. As she descended, her heel would catch on her hem. Two steps from the bottom, she'd trip, but there would be no Nic to catch her. He was surrounded by five women each vying for his attention. Without him to save her, she would make a grab for the banister and miss.

Flashes would explode in her eyes like fireworks as dozens of press cameras captured her ignominy at a hundred frames per second.

"Dr. Davis?" Libby peered at her in concern. "Is something amiss?"

Brooke shook herself out of the horrifying daydream and swallowed the lump that had appeared in her throat. "Call me Brooke. This is—" Her gaze roved around the space as maids bustled past with vases of flowers and two well-dressed gentlemen strode by carrying briefcases and speaking in low tones. "Really big. And very beautiful," she rushed to add.

"Come. Princess Olivia is in her office."

Normally nervous energy would have prompted Brooke to chatter uncontrollably. But as she followed Libby past the stairs and into a corridor, she was too overwhelmed. They walked past half a dozen rooms and took a couple more turns. In seconds, her sense of direction had completely failed her.

"You really know your way around." She'd lost the battle with her nerves. "How long have you worked in the palace?"

"A few months. I arrived with Princess Olivia."

"Be honest. How long did it take until you no longer got lost?"

Libby shot a wry smile over her shoulder. "Three weeks."

"I'm only expecting to be here a couple days. I don't suppose there's a map or something."

"I'm afraid not. And I was under the impression that you'd be with us until after the wedding."

Brooke stumbled as she caught the edge of her sandal on the marble floor. "That's not what Nic and I agreed to." But in fact, she wasn't sure if they'd discussed the length of her stay. It certainly couldn't stretch to include a royal wedding.

"I could be mistaken," Libby told her, turning into an open doorway.

The office into which Brooke stepped was decorated in feminine shades of cream and peach, but the functional layout spoke of productivity. On her entrance, a stunning blonde looked up from her laptop and smiled.

"You must be Dr. Davis," the woman exclaimed, rising to greet her. She held out a manicured hand. "Lovely to meet you. I'm Olivia Alessandro."

"It's nice to meet you, as well." The urge to curtsy overwhelmed Brooke and only the knowledge that she'd fall flat on her face if she tried kept her from acting like an idiot. "Your Highness."

"Oh, please call me Olivia. You're Nic's friend and that makes you like family."

It was impossible not to relax beneath Olivia's warm smile. "Please call me Brooke. I have to tell you that I'm a little overwhelmed to be here. This morning I was on a Greek island with no real destination in mind. And then Nic informs me that he intends to bring me to Sherdana."

"Something tells me he didn't plan much in advance, either." The way Olivia shook her head gave Brooke the impression that the future queen of Sherdana believed strongly in preparation and organization.

"Your secretary mentioned something about me staying until after your wedding," Brooke said, perching on the edge of the cream brocade chair Olivia gestured her into. "But I think it would be better if I caught a flight to California as soon as possible."

"I'm sure that could be arranged, but couldn't you stay for a while and see a little of the country? Gabriel and I have plans to tour some of the vineyards in a couple days and it would be lovely if you and Nic could join us."

"As nice as that sounds…" Brooke trailed off. Never before had she hesitated to speak her mind, but being blunt with Nic's sister-in-law seemed the wrong thing to do. "I'm just worried about overstaying my welcome."

"Nonsense."

Brooke tried again. "I got the impression from Nic that his mother had arranged quite a few events in the next week or so that he's expected to attend. I wouldn't want to distract Nic from what he needs to do."

Olivia looked surprised. "You know why he came home?"

"He needs to get married so there can be…" It suddenly occurred to Brooke that the woman who was supposed to

produce Sherdana's next generation of heirs but couldn't
was seated across from her.

"It's okay." Olivia's smile was a study in tranquillity.
"I've made peace with what happened to me. And I consider myself the luckiest woman alive that Gabriel wanted
to marry me even though I wasn't the best choice for the
country."

"I think you're the perfect princess. Sherdana is damned
lucky to have you." Brooke grimaced at her less than elo-
quent language. "Sorry. I have a tendency to be blunt even
when I'm trying not to."

"Don't be sorry. It was a lovely compliment and I like
your directness. I can't wait for you to meet Ariana. She
has a knack for speaking her mind, as well."

"I saw her artwork at the villa. She's very talented. I'm
looking forward to talking with her about it."

"She's been vacationing with friends in Monaco for a
few days and is expected home late tonight. She's very
excited that you've come to visit. When I spoke with her
earlier today, she told me she'd met your brother when he
and Nic stayed at the villa."

That was something else Glen had neglected to mention. Brooke intended to have a long chat with her brother
when she returned to California.

"And now, I expect you would like to go to your room
and get settled. Dinner will be served at seven. If you need
anything let a maid know and she can get it for you."

Brooke gave a shaky laugh. "Like a whole new wardrobe? I'm afraid I packed to visit a Greek island. Casual
things." She imagined showing up to dinner in her tribal
print maxi and winced. "I really don't have anything I
could wear to dine in a palace."

"Oh." Olivia nodded. "I should have realized that from
the little Gabriel told me. It looks like you and I are the

same size, I'll send some things down for you to choose from."

Unsure whether to be horrified or grateful, Brooke could see protesting was foolish so she thanked Olivia. Then she followed a maid through the palace in a journey from the royal family's private wing to the rooms set aside for guest use. After five minutes of walking Brooke knew she'd never find her way back to Olivia's office and hoped someone would be sent to fetch her for dinner. If her presence in the palace was forgotten and she starved to death, how long would it take before her body was discovered? She lost count how many doors they passed before the maid stopped and gestured for Brooke to enter a room.

"Thank you."

The instant Brooke stepped into the bedroom she'd been given, she fell instantly in love. The wallpaper was a gold-and-white floral design while the curtains and bedding were a pale blue green that made her think of an Ameraucana chicken egg. In addition to a bed and a writing desk, the room held a settee and a small table flanked by chairs against the wall between two enormous windows. The room had enough furniture to comfortably seat the students in her class on Italian Renaissance poetry.

On the bench at the foot of her bed sat her well-worn luggage. To say it looked shabby among the opulent furnishings was an understatement.

"Can I unpack that for you, Dr. Davis?" The maid who'd brought Brooke here had followed her into the room.

"I've been traveling for quite a few days already and most of what's in here is dirty."

Brooke sensed that she would scandalize the maid by inquiring if there was a laundry machine she could use.

"I'll sort through everything and have it back to you by evening."

Brooke dug through the bag and pulled out her toiletries

and the notebook she always kept close by to write down the things that popped into her head. Her mother was fond of saying you never knew when inspiration would strike and some of Brooke's best ideas came when she was in the shower or grabbing a bite to eat.

Once the maid had left, Brooke picked up her cell phone and checked the time in California. At four o'clock in Sherdana it would be 7:00 a.m. in LA. Theresa would be halfway to work. Brooke dialed.

When Theresa answered, Brooke said, "Guess where I am now…"

Nic hadn't been in the palace more than fifteen minutes before his mother's private secretary tracked him down in the billiards room where he and Gabriel were drinking Scotch and catching up. The room had four enormous paintings depicting pivotal scenes in Sherdana's history, including the ratification of the 1749 constitution that was creating such chaos in Nic's personal life.

"Good afternoon, Your Highnesses." A petite woman in her midfifties stood just inside the door with her hands clasped at her waist.

Gwen had come to work for the queen as her personal assistant not long before the three princes had been born and more often than not, regarded the triplets as errant children rather than remarkable men.

"Hello, Gweny."

"None of that."

Nic crossed the room to kiss her cheek. "I missed you."

Her gaze grew even sterner, although a hint of softness developed near the edges of her lips. "You missed tea."

"I needed something a little stronger." Nic held up his mostly empty crystal tumbler.

"The queen expected you to attend her as soon as you arrived in the palace. She's in the rose garden. You'd better go immediately." Gwen's tone was a whip, driving him from the room.

Knowing better than to dawdle, Nic went straight outside and found his mother in her favorite part of the garden. Thanks to the queen's unwavering devotion, the half acre flourished with a mixture of difficult-to-find antique rose varieties as well as some that had been recently engineered to produce an unusual color or enhanced fragrance.

"It's about time you got around to saying hello," the queen declared, peering at him from beneath the wide brim of her sun hat.

"Good afternoon, Mother." Nic kissed the cheek his mother offered him and fell into step beside her. He didn't bother to offer her an explanation of what he'd been doing. She had no tolerance for excuses. "The roses look beautiful."

"I understand you brought a girl home with you. She's the sister of your California friend." She paused only briefly before continuing, obviously not expecting Nic to confirm what she'd said. "What is your relationship to her?"

"We're friends."

"Don't treat me like an idiot. I need to know if she's going to present a problem."

"No." At least not to anyone but him.

"Does she understand that you have come home to find a wife?"

"She does. It's not an issue. She's planning on heading home after the wedding."

"I understand you are taking her along with Gabriel and Olivia on a trip to the vineyards?"

"Gabriel mentioned something about it, but I haven't spoken with Brooke."

"I don't think it's a good idea that you get any more involved with this girl than you already are."

"We're not involved," Nic assured her.

"Is she in love with you?" Nic waited too long to answer and his mother made a disgusted sound. "Do you love her?"

"It doesn't matter how we feel about each other," Nic said, his voice tense and impatient. "I know my duty to Sherdana and nothing will get in the way of that." From his conversation with Gabriel, Nic knew she hadn't gone this hard at Christian. Why was Nic alone feeling the pressure to marry? Christian was just as much a prince of Sherdana. His son could just as easily rule. "I assume you have several matrimonial candidates for me to consider."

"I've sent their dossiers to your room in the visitors' wing. Did Gabriel mention the problem in your suite earlier today? Apparently your bathtub overflowed and flooded the room."

"Gabriel thought it might have been the twins although no one caught them at it."

His mother shook her head. "I don't know why we're paying a nanny if the girl can't keep track of them."

"From what I understand they are a handful."

"There are only two of them. I had three of you to contend with." His mother took Nic's hand in hers and squeezed hard. "It's good to have you home." She blinked rapidly a few times and released her grip on him. "Now, run along and look over the files I sent to your room. I expect you to share your thoughts with me after dinner tonight."

"Of course." He bent and kissed her cheek again. "First I'm off to see Father. I understand he has a ten-minute gap in his schedule shortly before five."

After reconnecting briefly with his father, Nic headed to the room he'd been given until his suite could be dried out. The oddity of the incident left him shaking his head.

How could a pair of two-year-old girls be as much trouble as everyone said?

As his mother had promised, a pile of dossiers had been left on the desk. Shrugging out of his blazer, Nic picked up the stack and counted. There were eight. He had twenty minutes before the tailor arrived to measure him for a whole new wardrobe. The clothes he'd traveled in today had belonged to Christian, as had most of what he'd worn the past ten days. Of the three brothers, Christian spent the most time at the Greek villa.

Nic settled into a chair in front of the unlit fireplace and selected a file at random. The photo clipped to the inside showed a stunning brunette with vivacious blue eyes and full lips. She was the twenty-five-year-old daughter of an Italian count, had gotten her MBA at Harvard and now worked for a global conglomerate headquartered in Paris. She spoke four languages and was admired for being fashionable as well as active on the charity circuit. In short, she was perfect.

He dropped the file onto the floor at his feet and opened the next one. This one was a blonde. Again beautiful. British born. The sister of a viscount. A human rights lawyer.

The next. Brunette. Pretty with big brown eyes and an alluring smile. A local girl. Her family owned the largest winery in Sherdana. She played cello for the Vienna Philharmonic.

Then another blonde. Bewitching green eyes. Daughter of a Danish baron. A model and television personality.

On and on. Each woman strikingly beautiful, accomplished and with a flawless pedigree.

Nic felt like a prize bull.

Replaying the conversation with his mother, he recognized he shouldn't have ignored Brooke's concerns that their relationship would come under scrutiny. He'd deliberately underestimated his mother's perceptiveness. But he didn't regret bringing Brooke to meet his family.

What he wasn't so happy about, however, was how little time they would have together in the days between now and her eventual departure. Being forced by propriety to keep his distance would be much more difficult now that he'd opened the door to what could have been if only he wasn't bound to his country.

At the same moment he threw the last folder onto the floor, a knock sounded on his door. Calling permission to enter, Nic got to his feet and scooped up the dossiers, depositing them back on the desk before turning to face the tailor and his small army of assistants who were to dress Nic.

While the suits he tried on were marked and pinned, Nic fell to thinking about Brooke. He hadn't seen her since leaving the plane and wondered how she'd coped in the hours they'd been apart. Despite the nervousness she'd shown during the flight, he suspected she'd figured out a way to charm everyone she'd encountered. He knew she was supposed to meet with Gabriel's wife right away and wondered how that had gone.

He was eager to meet Olivia. He already knew she was beautiful, intelligent and a strong crusader for children's health and welfare. The citizens loved her and after the drama surrounding her emergency hysterectomy and her subsequent secret elopement with Gabriel so did the media. But Nic was fascinated by how she'd caused such drastic changes in his brother.

The tailor finished his preliminary work and departed. Alone once more, Nic dressed for dinner. Family evenings were for the most part casual and Nic left his room wearing navy slacks and a crisp white shirt he'd purchased at a department store in California. His fashionable younger brother would be appalled that Nic was dressing *off the rack.* Nic was smiling at the thought as he joined Gabriel and his new bride in the family's private drawing room.

"You've made my brother a very happy man," Nic told Olivia, kissing her cheek in greeting. "I haven't seen him smile this much since we were children."

From her location snuggled beneath her husband's possessive arm, the blonde stared up at Gabriel with eyes filled with such love that a knot formed in Nic's gut. At that instant, any lingering resentment he'd felt at the uncomfortable position Gabriel's choice had put him in vanished. His brother deserved to be happy. The responsibility of the country would one day rest on Gabriel's shoulders and being married to the woman he loved would make his burden lighter.

This drew Nic's thoughts back to the dossiers in his room. He was glad there hadn't been a redhead among them. Brooke was a singular marvel in his mind. Marrying a woman with similar hair color was out of the question. He couldn't spend the rest of his life wishing his wife's red hair framed a different face.

Brooke hadn't made an appearance by the time Nic's parents entered the drawing room and he wondered for one brief moment if she'd let her anxiety get the better of her. He was seconds away from sending a maid to check on her when the door opened and Brooke stumbled in, unsteady in heels that appeared too large for her.

She wore a long-sleeved, gold, lace dress that flattered her curves, but conflicted with her usual carefree style. She wasn't wearing her usual long necklace that drew attention to the swell of her breasts, and she'd left her collection of bracelets behind. The look was sophisticated, elegant and formal, except for her hair, which spiraled and bounced around her shoulders like a living thing.

"Dr. Davis, welcome." Gabriel and Olivia had approached her while Nic stood there gaping at her transformation.

"I'm so sorry I'm late," Brooke was saying as he finally approached. "I only meant to close my eyes for fifteen minutes. Then next thing I know it's six-thirty. Thank heavens I showered before I sacked out. Of course this is what happens to my hair when I just let it go. If I'd had a few more minutes, I could have done something to it but I had such a hard time deciding which dress to wear. They were all so beautiful."

"You look lovely." Olivia gave her a warm smile and drew her arm through Brooke's in a show of affection and support. "Why don't I introduce you to Gabriel and Nic's parents."

"You mean the king and queen?" Brooke whispered, her gaze shooting to the couple enjoying a predinner cocktail. They appeared to be ignoring the knot of young people.

"They are eager to meet you," Gabriel said.

Brooke's lips quirked in a wry smile. "That's sweet of you to say." She took a clumsy step and smiled apologetically at Olivia. "I'm usually less awkward than this."

"The shoes are a little large for you," Olivia said, giving the gold laser-cut pumps a critical look. "I didn't realize your feet were so much smaller than mine. Perhaps you have something of your own that would fit better? I could send a maid to fetch something."

"Are you kidding me?" Brooke retorted, her voice feverish as she took her next step with more deliberation and improved grace. "These are *Louboutin glass slippers*. I'm Cinderella."

Gabriel waited a beat before following his wife. He caught Nic's eye and smirked. "I like her."

"So do I," Nic replied, his voice low and subdued.

Not that it should have mattered to Nic, but his brother's words sent gratitude and relief rushing into his chest. It was good to know he had at least two people in the palace, Gabriel and Olivia, who would understand how wretched doing the right thing could feel.

"It's very nice to meet you," Brooke was saying to his parents as Nic and Gabriel caught up to the women. "Thank you for letting me stay at the palace for a few days."

Nic felt the impact of his mother's gaze as he drew up beside Brooke. He set his palm on her back and through her dress felt the tension quivering in her muscles.

"We are happy to have you," Nic's father said, his broad smile genuine.

When it came to matters affecting his country, the king was a mighty warrior defending his realm from all threats social, economic and diplomatic. However, he was a teddy bear when it came to his wife and children. But the queen ruled her family with an iron fist in a velvet glove. All four of her children knew the strength of her will and respected it. In exchange she allowed them the opportunity to figure out their place in the world.

This meant Nic had been allowed to attend university in the United States and stay there living his dream of space travel until Sherdana had needed him to come home. But while he'd appreciated his ten years of freedom from responsibility, it made his return that much harder.

"Very happy," the queen echoed. "I understand, Miss Davis, that you are the sister of the man Nic has been working with for the last five years."

"Yes, my brother is in charge of the *Griffin* project."

"Perhaps you will join me for breakfast tomorrow. I'd like to hear more about the project Nic has been working on with your brother."

"I would be happy to have breakfast with you."

"Wonderful. Is eight o'clock too early for you?"

"Not at all. Unlike Nic, I'm an early riser."

Nic knew she'd meant the jab for him. It was an old joke between them on the mornings when he'd worked late into the night and then crashed on the couch in his workroom. But he could see at once that his mother was wondering how Brooke knew what time Nic got out of bed in the morning.

Even without glancing toward his brother, Gabriel's amusement was apparent. Nic kept his own expression bland as he met his mother's steely gaze.

Olivia saved the moment from further awkwardness. "And after breakfast perhaps you could come to the stables and watch the twins take a riding lesson. They are showing great promise as equestrians. Do you ride, Brooke?"

"I did when I was younger, but school has kept me far too busy in recent years."

"Brooke has two doctorates," Nic interjected smoothly. "She teaches Italian language and literature at the University of California, Santa Cruz."

"You're young to have accomplished that much," Gabriel said.

Brooke nodded. "I graduated high school with two years of college credits and spent the next ten years immersed in academia. After my brother went off to college my parents hosted a girl from Italy. She stayed with us a year and by the time she went home, I was fluent in Italian and learning to read it, as well."

Olivia spoke up. "Have you spent much time in Italy?"

"While I was working on my second doctorate, I spent a year in Florence and Rome. Before that my mother and I would visit for a week or two during the summer depending on her deadlines. She writes for television and has penned a mystery series set in sixteenth-century Venice that does very well." Talking about her mother's accomplishments had relaxed Brooke. Her eyes sparkled with pride.

This relaxed Nic as well, but as the family made their way toward the dining room, the queen pulled him aside.

"Lovely girl, your Miss Davis."

"Actually it's Dr. Davis." Although he had a feeling his mother already knew that and had spoken incorrectly to get a rise out of her son. And since Nic had already denied that he and Brooke were anything but friends, why did his mother put the emphasis on *your*? "I'm glad you like her."

"Did you look at the files I gave you?"

"Yes. Any one of them would be a fine princess." He couldn't bring himself to use the word *wife* yet. "You and your team did a fine job of choosing candidates that lined up with my needs."

"Yes we did. Now, let's see if you can do an equally fine job choosing a wife."

Nine

At her first dinner with Nic's family, Brooke sat beside Nic on the king's left hand and ate little. Part of the reason she'd been late to dinner was another bout of nausea that struck her shortly after she'd risen. So much for morning sickness. Brooke wasn't sure why it was called that when it seemed to strike her at random times throughout the day.

"You're not eating," Nic murmured, the first words he'd spoken directly to her since the meal had begun.

"I'm dining with royalty," she muttered back. "My stomach is in knots."

"They're just people."

"Important people." Wealthy, sophisticated, intelligent people. "Normally I wouldn't get unsettled by this sort of thing, but this is your family and I want them to like me."

"I assure you they do."

"Sure." Brooke resisted the urge to roll her eyes. His mother had been observing her through most of the meal, making each swallow of the delicious salmon more trial than pleasure. Brooke sensed that the queen had a long list of questions she wanted to ask, starting with: When are you going home? Not that Brooke blamed her. Nic's mother had plans for her son. Plans that she must perceive as being threatened by an uncouth redhead who regarded Nic with adoring eyes.

Despite the fact that the meal was a relaxed family affair and not the formal ordeal Brooke had feared, by the time the dessert course concluded, she was more than ready to escape. She was relieved, therefore, when Gabriel and Olivia offered her a quick tour of the public areas of the palace before escorting her back to her room.

Strolling the hall of portraits, Brooke realized the extent of Sherdana's history. Some of the paintings dated back to the late-fifteenth century. Thanks to all those years when she'd accompanied her mother to Italy and helped her research the Italian Renaissance period, Brooke had developed a love of history that partially explained why she'd chosen the same time period for her second doctorate.

"I imagine you have a library with books on Sherdana's history," she said to Gabriel as he and Olivia led the way to the ballroom.

"An extensive one. We'll make that our next stop."

A half an hour later the trio arrived at Brooke's door. She was feeling a touch giddy at the idea that she could return to the library the next day and check out the collection more thoroughly. The vast amount of books contained in the two-story room was an academic's dream come true. She could probably spend an entire year in Sherdana's palace library and never need to leave.

"Thank you for the tour."

"You are very welcome," Olivia said. "If you need anything else tonight, let one of the maids know. There is always someone on call."

Brooke bid the prince and princess good-night and entered her room. As she did, she noticed the store of crackers she'd nibbled on prior to dinner had been replenished. With a grateful sigh, Brooke grabbed a handful and went to the wardrobe. As the maid had promised earlier, her clothes had been laundered and returned. Brooke grinned as she slipped off her borrowed shoes, guessing the staff wasn't accustomed to washing ragged denim shorts and cotton peasant blouses. Regardless, they'd done a marvelous job. Her clothes looked brand-new.

A knock sounded on her door. Brooke's pulse kicked up. Could Nic have come by to wish her good-night? But it wasn't her handsome prince in the hall. Instead, her visitor was a beautiful, tall girl with long chocolate-brown hair and a welcoming smile.

"I'm Ariana." Behind Nic's sister were two maids loaded down with six shoe boxes and four overstuffed garment bags.

"Brooke Davis."

"I know that." Ariana laughed. "Even if the palace wasn't buzzing about the girl Nic brought home, I would have recognized you from the pictures Glen emailed me from time to time. He's very proud of you."

"You and Glen email?" Earlier Brooke had learned that Nic's sister had met Glen in Greece, but an ongoing correspondence was something else entirely. "I thought you'd just met the one time."

"Yeees." She drew the word out. "But it was *quite* a meeting."

Brooke didn't know what to make of the other girl's innuendo and made a note to question Glen about Nic's sister.

"Olivia told me her shoes were too big for you, so I brought you a few pairs of mine," Ariana said, indicating the maids behind her. "They should fit you better—and I included some dresses, as well. That's one of Olivia's, isn't it?"

Brooke couldn't figure out what about the gold lace could possibly have caused Ariana to wrinkle her nose. "Nothing I brought with me is suitable for palace wear. I had no plans to come here with Nic."

For a moment Ariana's eyes narrowed in the same sharp expression of assessment her mother had aimed at Brooke all evening. At last the princess smiled. "Well, I'm glad you did."

"So am I." And for the first time in eight hours, Brooke meant it. "I've really been looking forward to meeting you. I thought your artwork at the villa was amazing."

"Then you'd be the first." With a self-deprecating hair flip, Ariana slipped her arm through Brooke's and drew her into the bedroom.

"What do you mean?" Brooke let herself be led. From the way Nic had talked about his sister and from studying Ariana's art, Brooke felt as if she and the younger woman might be kindred spirits. "Your use of color gave the paintings such energy and depth."

Ariana's eyebrows drew together. "You're serious." She sounded surprised and more than a little hopeful.

"Very." Brooke didn't understand the princess's reaction. "I did my undergrad work in visual and critical studies."

"My family doesn't understand what I paint. They see it all as random splashes of color on canvas."

"I'm sure it's just that they are accustomed to a more traditional style of painting. Have you ever had your work exhibited anywhere?"

"No." A laugh bubbled out of her. "I paint for myself."

"Of course. But if you're ever interested in getting an expert's opinion, I have a friend in San Francisco who runs a gallery. He likes finding new talent. I took some pictures of your work. With your permission I could send him the photos."

"I've never thought…" Ariana shook her head in bemusement. "I guess this is the moment every artist faces at some point. Do I take a chance and risk failing or play it safe and never know if I'm any good."

"Oh, you're good," Brooke assured her. "But art is very subjective and not everyone is going to like what you do."

"I guess I've already faced my worst critics. My family. So why not see what your friend thinks."

"Wonderful, I'll send him the pictures tomorrow morning."

"And in the meantime—" Ariana gestured toward the wardrobe "—show me what you brought from home and let's see if I have anything that will appeal to you."

Brooke suspected the stylish princess wouldn't be at all impressed with the limited contents of her closet, but she knew her fine speech about art being subjective would be hypocritical if she couldn't back it up with action. For what was fashion but wearable art and even though Brooke's wardrobe wasn't suitable for a palace, it worked perfectly in her academic world.

The maids who'd entered behind Ariana deposited their burdens on Brooke's bed. If the princess had brought anything like what she was wearing—a sophisticated but fun plum dress with gold circles embroidered around the neckline and dotted over the skirt—Brooke braced herself to be wowed.

"It feels like every day is Christmas around here," Brooke said as dress after gorgeous dress came free of the garment bags. The variety of colors and styles dazzled Brooke. Of course, with her skin tone, Ariana could wear just about anything.

When the maids finished, Brooke pulled out her own dresses, shorts, skirts and her favorite kimono. Ariana narrowed her eyes in thought and surveyed each item.

"You have a great eye for color and know exactly what suits you."

Coming from the princess, this was a huge compliment. Ariana wasn't at all what Brooke imagined a princess would be like. She was warm and approachable. Not at all stuffy or formal. Brooke warmed to her quickly, feeling as if they had known each other for years instead of minutes.

"In California I blend in dressed like this." Brooke slipped into the tie-dyed kimono. It looked odd over the gold lace dress she'd borrowed from Olivia. "Here I stick out like a sore thumb."

"Hardly a sore thumb, although definitely a standout. No matter how you dress, your unique hair color will keep you from being a wallflower. No wonder my brother finds you irresistible."

Brooke felt Ariana's comment like a blow. "We're just friends," she explained in a rush, but her cheeks heated as the princess arched one slim eyebrow.

"But he talks about you all the time and he brought you to meet us."

"It's not what you're thinking. I went to the island to convince him to return to California. To Glen and the *Griffin* project. And when he was summoned back here sooner than expected, he didn't want to leave me alone in Greece."

"He must be in love with you. He's never brought a woman home before."

Brooke relaxed a little. "That's because the love of his life wouldn't fit inside an airplane." Seeing she had confused Ariana, Brooke explained. "As long as I've known him, Nic has been committed to the rocket he and my brother hope will one day carry people into space. There's been no room for an emotional connection with any woman."

"And yet here you are."

"Until a few days ago I didn't know he was a prince or that he needs to marry a citizen of the country or an aristocrat so his children can rule someday. Obviously I'm neither."

"He wouldn't have kept something like that from you unless he was worried about hurting you."

"That much is true." Here Brooke hesitated, unsure how much to explain. In the end, she decided to trust Ariana. "I've had a crush on him for years. When I showed up on Ithaca, he told me everything. He didn't want me to hope for a future we could never have together."

"Did it work? Did you stop hoping?"

"I'd be crazy if I didn't."

Like her brothers, Ariana had her father's warm brown eyes flecked with gold, but she'd inherited the intensity of her gaze from her mother. "But you two have been intimate."

Hating to lie, Brooke pretended she hadn't heard the soft question. Instead she chose a dress at random and announced, "I love this."

Luckily her selection was a flirty emerald-green dress that she could see herself wearing. Brooke held it against her body. As she looked at her reflection, she noticed the dress had no tags, but Brooke doubted it had ever been worn.

"I'll take your nonanswer as an affirmative." Ariana's musical laughter filled the room. "Try on the dress." While Brooke obeyed her, the princess continued, "I'm sorry if I was blunt and please don't be embarrassed." The gold bracelets on her slender wrists chimed. "My brothers are very hard for the opposite sex to resist. Thank goodness Gabriel and Nic are honorable and not ones to take advantage. Christian is like a child in a toy store wanting everything he sees."

And getting it, too, Brooke guessed. "Please don't tell

anyone about Nic and me. It's over and I wouldn't want to cause any needless problems."

Ariana nodded. "That dress is amazing on you."

The empire bodice cupped her breasts, the fabric ending in a narrow band of a darker green ribbon. From there, the layers of chiffon material flowed over her hips, the hem ending just above her knee. Brooke stared at herself in the mirror as Ariana guided her feet into strappy black sandals.

"It brings out the green in your eyes."

"I feel like a princess." Brooke laughed. "I guess I should because it's a dress fit for a princess. You."

Next, Ariana urged Brooke into a hot-pink sheath with a V-shaped neckline and bands of fabric that crisscrossed diagonally to create an interesting and figure-slimming pattern. It had a sophisticated, elegant vibe that Brooke wasn't sure she could pull off.

"I understand you are having breakfast with my mother tomorrow. This will be perfect, and I think you should pair it with these."

Ariana grabbed a box and pulled out a pair of white suede and black velvet lace ankle boots that were amazing, Brooke waved her hands in protest. "I can't. Those are just too much."

"You must wear them or the outfit will not be complete."

At Ariana's relentless urging, Brooke slipped her feet into the boots and faced the mirror, accepting immediately that she'd lost the battle. "I never imagined I could look like this."

Ariana's eyebrows lifted in surprise. "Why not? You are very beautiful."

"But not refined and effortless like you and Olivia."

With a very unladylike snort, Ariana rolled her eyes. "This is just how I appear here in the palace. When I go to Ithaca, I assure you, I'm so different you'd never recognize me."

"Do you spend a lot of time on the island?"

"Not as much as I'd like. It's an escape. I go to paint. To forget about the responsibilities of being a princess."

"I imagine there's a lot that keeps you busy."

"It's less now that Olivia is here." Ariana selected five more dresses and put them into Olivia's wardrobe with three more pairs of shoes. "That will do for now, but you will need a long dress for a party we must attend the day after tomorrow. It's the prime minister's birthday."

"Are you sure I will be going?"

"Absolutely. The event is always deadly dull and having you along will make the whole thing bearable."

While the maids returned the rest of the dresses to the garment bags, Ariana squeezed Brooke's shoulder. "I am sorry you and Nic cannot see where things might lead between you. I think you would make him very happy."

"Actually, I drive him crazy."

"Good. He has always been too serious. He needs a little crazy in his life." And with that, Ariana said good-night and left Brooke to her thoughts.

The corridors of the visitors' wing were quiet as Nic made his way back to his temporary quarters. The tranquillity would vanish over the next few days as guests began to arrive for the week of festivities leading up to the royal wedding. The conversation he'd had with his parents after dinner had highlighted their expectations for him. The women in the dossiers had been invited to the palace. He was to get to know each of them and make his selection.

As he'd listened to his mother, Nic realized he'd been in America too long. Although he'd grown up in a world where marriages sometimes were arranged, he'd grown accustomed to the notion of dating freely without any expectation that it might end in marriage.

He'd almost reached his suite when the door to the room

beside his opened and two maids emerged carrying garment bags. Their appearance could only mean he had company next door. It hadn't occurred to Nic that Brooke had been placed on this floor, much less in the room beside his, and his suspicion was confirmed when his sister came out of the room a few seconds later.

"Nic!" She raced across the few feet that separated them and threw herself into his arms. "How good that you're home."

She smelled of the light floral perfume he'd sent her the previous Christmas. He'd asked Brooke to help him pick out the perfume because he'd sensed the two women were a lot alike. Seeing his sister's good mood upon leaving Brooke, he knew he'd been right.

"I'm happy to be here."

Ariana pushed back until she could see his expression, and then clicked her tongue. "No you're not. You'd much rather be in California playing with your rocket."

"I'm done with that." The accident and Gabriel's marriage had seen to that.

"It's not like you to give up."

Her remark sent a wave of anger rushing through him. The emotion was so sharp and so immediate that he could do nothing more than stand frozen in astonishment. The loss of *Griffin*. His obligation to give up his dream and come home to marry a woman he didn't love. None of it was of his choosing.

But without this call to duty, would he have stayed in California and started over? The accident had been a disaster and his confidence was in shreds. Was that why he wasn't fighting his fate or figuring out a way around the laws that were in place so he could choose whom he married?

"Nic?"

As quickly as it had risen, his rage subsided. He shook

himself in the numb aftermath. "Sorry. I'm just tired. It's been a long day. And I didn't give up." He gave her nose an affectionate tweak the way he used to when she was an adorable toddler and he an oh-so-knowing big brother of ten. "I was called home to do my duty."

Ariana winced. "You're right. I'm sorry." Her contrite expression vanished with her next breath. "I met Brooke tonight. She's wonderful."

He was starting to wish his siblings would find something about Brooke to criticize. It was going to be hell bidding her goodbye and it would have been easier on him if they behaved as if falling for her was a huge error in his judgment.

"I'm glad you think so."

"If you're going to visit her, you might want to hurry. I think she was getting ready for bed."

For a second Nic wasn't sure if he should take his sister's statement at face value or if she was trying to get a reaction out of him. He decided it was the latter.

"This is my room." He indicated the door to his left. "I didn't know where she was staying in the palace."

"Why are you in the visitors' wing?"

"Something about my room flooding."

She gave him an incredulous look. "Who told you that?"

"Gabriel." Nic was starting to suspect something might be up. "Why?"

"Because I stopped by your suite earlier and it looked fine to me." She smirked. "I think our brother is trying to play matchmaker. You and Brooke all alone in the visitors' wing with no one to know if you snuck into each other's rooms. Very romantic."

"Damn it." Now he had another dilemma facing him. Confront Gabriel and return to his suite in the family wing or pretend he and Ariana never had this conversation and do what his heart wanted but his brain protested against.

"Honestly, stop being so noble." It was as if Ariana had read his mind. "Gabriel followed his heart. I think he wants the same for you."

"And then who will produce the legitimate heirs to ascend the throne?"

His sister shrugged. "There's always Christian. He isn't in love with anyone. Let him be the sacrificial lamb."

Nic hugged his sister and kissed the top of her head. "You are the best sister in the world."

"So are you going to choose Brooke?"

"You know I can't and you know why."

With a huge sigh, Ariana pushed him away. "You are too honorable for your own good."

"I know how this whole thing is making me feel. I can't do that to Christian." He paused and looked down at her. "Or to you."

"Me?"

"Have you considered what would happen if both Christian and I failed to produce a son? The whole burden shifts to your shoulders."

Ariana obviously hadn't considered this. Even though the constitution wouldn't allow her to rule as queen, she was still a direct descendant of the ruling king and that meant her son could one day succeed.

"Okay, I see your point, but I think it's terrible that you and Brooke can't be together."

"So do I."

Nic watched as his sister retreated down the corridor. For several heartbeats he stood with his hand on the doorknob to his room, willing himself to open the door and step inside, while Ariana's words rang in his head. *Brooke was getting ready for bed.* They were isolated in this wing of the palace. He could spend the night with her and sneak out before anyone discovered them. But how many times could he tell himself this was their last time together? Just that morning he'd been on the verge of saying goodbye.

He pushed open the door to his room, but didn't step across the threshold. He'd invited Brooke to Sherdana; it would only be polite to stop by and find out how her day had gone. If he stood in the hall, they could have a quick conversation without fear that either of them would be overcome with passion. That decided, Nic strode over and rapped on Brooke's door. If he'd expected her to answer his summons looking disheveled and adorable in her pajamas, he was doomed to disappointment.

The stylish creature that stood before him was nothing like the Brooke he'd grown accustomed to. Even the dress she'd worn at dinner tonight, as beautiful as she'd looked in it, hadn't stretched his perception of her as much as this strapless pale pink ball gown that turned her into a Disney princess.

Obviously enjoying herself, Brooke twirled twice and then paused for his opinion. "What do you think?"

"That's quite a dress."

She laughed, a bright silvery sound he hadn't heard since before the day he'd put an end to their fledgling romance. His heart lifted at her joy.

"I never imagined dressing like a princess would be so much fun."

His gut clenched at her words. She didn't mean them the way they'd sounded. The last thing she'd ever do was pick on him for rejecting her as unsuitable. Brooke wasn't the sort to play games or come at a problem sideways. It was one of the things he appreciated about her.

But that didn't stop regret from choking him.

"You look incredibly beautiful."

She shot him a flirtatious grin. "Aw, you're just saying that because it's true. Ariana brought the dress. I simply had to try it on since I'll never get the chance to wear it in public."

"Why not?"

"We both know the answer to that."

She drew him into the room and closed the door. Her actions had a dangerous effect on Nic's libido. He really hadn't come to her suite to make love to her, but it wouldn't take more than another one of her delicious smiles for him to snatch her into his arms and carry her to the bed.

"I don't think I follow you," Nic said, crossing his arms over his chest, his gaze tracking her every move as she enjoyed her reflection. He caught himself smiling as she shifted from side to side to make the skirt swish.

"Your mother and I are having breakfast tomorrow. I'm certain she's going to politely but firmly give me the heave-ho."

"She'd never be that rude."

"Of course not. But she can't be happy that her son brought home some inappropriate girl when he's supposed to be focused on selecting a bride."

"You're not inappropriate."

"I am where your future is concerned." Brooke reached for the dress's side zipper and gave Nic a stern look. "Turn around. I need to get out of this dress."

Blood pounded in his ears. "You are aware that I've seen you naked many, many times."

"That was before I was staying beneath your parents' roof. I think it would be rude of us to take advantage of their hospitality by getting swept up in a passionate moment. Don't you?" She set her hands on her hips. "So, turn around."

"My not watching you strip out of your clothes isn't going to prevent us from getting swept up in a passionate moment. I have memorized every inch of your gorgeous body."

"Turn around." Although her color was high, her firm tone deterred further argument.

At last Nic did as she'd asked. For several minutes the only sound in the room was the slide and crinkle of fabric as she undressed and the harsh rasp of his breath. He berated himself for acquiescing. If she was going to return to California in a few days, they were fools not to steal every moment they could to be together.

Bursting with conviction, Nic started to turn back around. "Brooke, we should…" He didn't finish because she gave him a sharp shove toward the door.

"No we shouldn't."

"One kiss." The irony of his demand wasn't lost on Nic. How many times had she teased, tormented and begged for any little bit of attention from him over the years? Time after time he'd refused her. "I missed waking up with you this morning."

"Whose fault was that?"

"Mine." It was all his fault. The five years when they could have been together if he hadn't been so obsessively focused on work. The way he'd hurt her because he'd chosen duty to his country over her. The emotional intimacy he couldn't give her because he was afraid his heart would break if he opened up.

"One kiss." He was pleading now.

"Fine. But you need to be in the hall with your hands behind your back."

A muscle ticked in his cheek. If she wanted to be in control, he would do his best to let that happen. "Agreed," he said and stepped out of her room.

Given the way he'd yielded to her conditions, Nic expected more demands from her.

"Close your eyes. I can't do this with you glaring at me."

In perfect stillness she waited him out. At last Nic let his lashes drift down. Years of working toward a single possibly unattainable goal would have been impossible without a great deal of fortitude, but Nic had recently discovered a shortage of patience where Brooke was concerned.

"Dear Nic." Her fingertips swept into his hair and tugged his head downward until their lips met.

Sweetness.

The tenderness of her kiss sent his heartbeat into overdrive. The desire previously driving through his body eased beneath her gentle touch. For the first time he acknowledged what existed between them wasn't born out of passion alone, but had its origins in something far deeper and lasting. A sigh fluttered in his chest as she lifted her lips from his and grazed them across his cheek.

"Good night, sweet prince."

Before he'd recovered enough to open his eyes, she was gone.

Ten

Thanks to Ariana's help with her wardrobe, Brooke had gone to bed feeling confident about her breakfast meeting with the queen. However, when she woke at dawn plagued by the increasingly familiar nausea, she plodded through her morning routine, burdened by anxiety.

By the time she'd swept her straightened hair into a smooth French roll, Brooke had consumed half a package of crackers in an effort to calm her roiling stomach. It seemed to be working because by the time she finished applying mascara and lipstick, she was feeling like her old self.

A maid appeared promptly at ten minutes to eight and Brooke dredged up her polite interview face as she followed her downstairs and into the garden. The girl pointed to a grassy path that curved past flower beds overflowing with shades of pink and purple. Brooke's destination—a white gazebo overlooking a small pond—appeared to be about fifty feet away. As she neared the structure, she noted that the queen had already arrived and was seated at the table placed in the center of the space. Rose-patterned china and crystal goblets were carefully arranged on a white tablecloth. The whole display reminded Brooke of a storybook tea party.

"Good morning, Your Majesty," Brooke said cheerfully as she neared.

The queen turned her attention from the electronic tablet in her hand and her keen gaze swept over Brooke, lingering for a long moment on the low boots. Brooke withstood the queen's assessment in silence, wondering if custom required her to curtsy.

"Hello, Dr. Davis. Don't you look lovely. Please sit down."

Noticing the change from last night in the way the queen addressed her, Brooke perched on the edge of a mint-green damask chair and dropped her napkin on her lap. Two maids stood by to wait on them. Brooke accepted a glass of orange juice and a cup of very dark coffee lightened with cream which she sipped until her stomach gurgled quietly. To cover the noise, Brooke began to speak.

"Your garden is beautiful." Ariana had offered Brooke several safe subjects on which to converse. "I understand you have several rare varieties of roses."

"Are you interested in gardening?" the queen asked, offering a polite smile. A diplomat's smile.

Brooke's whole digestive track picked that moment to complain. She pinched her lips tight in response. After a second she took a deep breath. "I love flowers, but I don't have much of a green thumb."

"I suppose you've been busy earning your two doctorates. That's quite impressive for someone your age." Most people thought it was impressive, period, but it made sense that the queen of a country would be hard to impress. "And now you teach at a university."

"Italian language and literature."

"Olivia tells me you've traveled around Italy quite a bit."

"As well as France, Austria and Switzerland. I love this part of the world."

"Have you ever wanted to live in Europe?"

At that moment Brooke wished she'd never agreed to come. Nic's mother obviously regarded her as an intruder, or worse, an opportunist. Should she explain that she understood Nic was off-limits? She couldn't imagine that was the sort of polite conversation one made with the elegant queen of Sherdana.

"I love California. I did my undergraduate work in New York City." Brooke knit her fingers together in her lap lest she surrender to the urge to play with her silverware. "I couldn't wait to get back home."

"Home is a wonderful place to be. Are you hungry?" The queen gestured to the maids and one of them lifted the lid off the serving dish. "Crepes are my weakness," the queen said. "There are also omelets made with spinach and mushrooms or the chef would be happy to prepare something else if you'd prefer."

"I don't want to be any trouble." The crepes looked marvelous. Some were filled with strawberries, others with something creamy and covered in apples or...

"Pears roasted in butter and honey over crepes filled with ricotta cheese," the queen said, her eyes softening for the first time in Brooke's company.

If Brooke hadn't been so queasy, she could have easily eaten her way through half a dozen of the thin fluffy pancakes. As it was, she took one of each kind and nibbled at them.

"Olivia tells me you spoke of leaving in the next few days," the queen remarked in her delightfully accented English. "But when I spoke with Nicolas last night, he wishes you to remain through the wedding." She tucked into her breakfast with relish, obviously enjoying herself. "I think my son believes himself in love with you."

Brooke's coffee cup rattled against the saucer as she set it down too abruptly. Her stomach seized and suddenly eating the crepes didn't strike her as the smartest idea. The queen's words repeated themselves several times in Brooke's head. *He believes himself in love with you.* Not *he's in love with you.* Brooke recognized the difference. In high school and college she'd believed herself in love any number of times. Then she'd met Nic and began the discovery of what love truly was.

"I'm sorry, but you're wrong." Brooke put her napkin to her lips as her body flushed hot. It wasn't embarrassment or guilt, but her system reacting to stress and being pregnant. "Nic knows his mind like no man I've ever met. His heart belongs to this country and his family."

The queen sighed. "And you are in love with him."

The edges of Brooke's vision darkened. What was Nic's mother trying to establish? Already Brooke had accepted that she and Nic had no future. She knew he would never give his mother any cause to believe otherwise so she guessed the queen's protective instincts were kicking in. She understood. In a little more than seven months she would have her own child to keep from harm. Heaven help anyone who got in her way.

"He's my brother's best friend…" Brooke said, her voice trailing off. "I've known Nic for years. Did I once want something more? Yes. But that was before I knew who he was and what was expected of him."

"Are you trying to tell me you didn't know he was a prince?"

Brooke held still beneath the queen's penetrating regard. The older woman's face became difficult to stay focused on. Brooke wanted nothing more than to lie down until the spinning stopped.

"I didn't know until a few days ago. He left California without a word after the accident. I tracked him down to Ithaca because he wouldn't return my phone calls or emails. I was worried about how he was coping in the aftermath." She hoped the queen was satisfied with her reason for following Nic to Greece and would refrain from probing further.

The queen nodded. "The rocket ship was very important to him. But it's gone and he needs to put it behind him." Her tone was matter-of-fact as she dismissed her son's driving passion.

"He can't just put it behind him. He feels responsible for the death of one of his fellow scientists." Brooke endured a sharp pinch of sadness that Nic's mother didn't understand this about her son. "Walter hadn't been with the team long, but he worked closely with Nic. I think part of the reason why Nic was so willing to come home and let you marry him off was because he felt as if he'd failed Walter and Glen and even you and the king. I think the reason he worked so hard was to justify being away from Sherdana. He spent every day proving that his work would benefit future generations, driving himself beyond exhaustion in order to contribute something amazing to the world. So that his absence from you had meaning."

Brooke didn't realize she'd gotten to her feet until the gazebo began to sway around her. She clamped a hand over her mouth as the unsettled feeling in her stomach increased. She couldn't throw up. Not now. Not here. Sweat broke out on her body. She was about to ruin Ariana's gorgeous dress in an inglorious way the palace would be talking about for weeks. Brooke blinked and gulped air to regain her equilibrium. But she was too hot. Too dizzy.

"I have to…" *Go.* She didn't belong here. She'd been unbearably rude to Nic's mother, who was the queen of a nation. But she could no longer tell in which direction lay escape.

"Dr. Davis, are you all right?" The queen sounded very far away.

Brooke tried to focus on the queen's voice but she stumbled. Abruptly a wood column was beneath her fingers and she clutched the rough surface like a lifeline as darkness rushed up to claim her.

Nic exploded through the green salon's French doors and raced toward the gazebo as soon as Brooke stood and began to weave like a drunken woman. For the past fifteen minutes he'd been positioned by the windows that overlooked the garden so he could observe the exchange between his mother and Brooke and step in if things appeared as if they were going badly. Like Brooke, he'd expected his mother to diplomatically encourage her to leave as soon as possible and he was worried that Brooke might say something she'd immediately regret. Never could he have predicted that he'd be just in time to catch Brooke's limp body before it hit the gazebo floor.

"What happened?"

For once his mother looked utterly confounded. "She was going on and on about you and the rocket and then she turned bright pink and collapsed."

Nic scooped Brooke into his arms and headed toward the palace. Whereas she'd been flushed a moment earlier, her skin was now deathly pale. He entered the green salon and crossed the room in several ground-eating strides. His heart hammered harder in his chest each time he glanced down at Brooke's unconscious face. What was wrong with her? As far as he recalled she'd been sick a mere handful of times and it had certainly never been this drastic. A cold. Sinus infection. Once a bad case of food poisoning.

He didn't realize his mother had followed him until he

pushed open the door to Brooke's suite and carried her to the bed.

"Is there something wrong with her that caused her to pass out?" the queen demanded, sitting on the bed to feel Brooke's skin. "She's clammy."

"She's perfectly healthy." He pulled out his phone, unsure if this was a true emergency. "She was anxious about coming here, but seemed all right at dinner last night. What did you say to her at breakfast? She seemed agitated before she passed out."

"You were watching us?"

"I was worried about how you two would get along. Seems I was right to be."

"I merely told her that I thought you believed yourself in love with her."

Nic closed his eyes briefly and shook his head. "What would possess you to tell her that?"

"I needed her to understand that what was between you wasn't real."

"How would you know? You barely know her and I haven't been around for ten years so you scarcely know me, either."

His mother looked shocked. "You are my son. I raised you."

With effort, Nic reeled in his temper. "None of this is helping Brooke. She hasn't awakened yet. I think she needs a doctor."

He was texting Gabriel when a single word from his mother stopped him.

"Wait."

"Why?"

She pointed at a package of crackers on the nightstand. "How long has she been eating these?"

"I have no idea." And what did it matter? "Do you think there's something wrong with them?"

"No, but when I was pregnant I used to eat crackers to fight nausea." His mother looked thoughtful. "She barely ate any of her dinner last night and she was picking at breakfast today. Pregnancy could explain her fainting spell."

"Pregnant?" Nic shook his head to clear the sudden rushing in his ears. "Impossible."

"Impossible because you haven't been intimate or because you thought you were being careful."

The blunt question shocked him for a moment before comprehension struck. Of course his mother knew he'd been involved with Brooke. They hadn't kept their relationship secret and no doubt Ariana had mentioned that he was seeing someone in California.

"We've been very careful."

"Then perhaps she has someone else in her life."

Nic glared at his mother. "There's no one else."

The queen pressed her lips together and didn't argue further. "I suggest we wait for her to come around and ask her. If there's something more serious going on, we can call the doctor then." His mother stood and smoothed her skirt. "I'll give you some privacy. Please let me know how she's doing when she wakes."

And with that, the queen left and Nic was alone with Brooke.

Pregnant.

With his child. The thought of it filled him with warmth. But all too quickly questions formed. Had she realized it yet? She wasn't showing and he guessed that she was between five and eight weeks along. Was that too early for her to suspect? Yet she'd obviously been queasy and had to wonder why.

Brooke began to stir and Nic went to sit beside her. She blinked and slowly focused on him.

"What happened?"

"You passed out."

"Damn." She rubbed her eyes. "I yelled at your mother. She must hate me."

"She doesn't." He skimmed his knuckles against her cheek. "What's going on with you? I've never known you to be sick."

She avoided his gaze. "Nothing, I'm just really over-wrought and I think my blood sugar is low because I was too nervous to eat much at dinner."

"Is that why you were eating these?" He picked up the crackers and held them before her.

"Whenever my stomach gets upset, I eat crackers to absorb the acid." Her words made sense, but something about her tone told him she wasn't giving him full disclosure.

"My mother told me she used to eat crackers when she was pregnant," he said. "She claimed it helped with nausea."

Brooke's body tensed. "I've heard that before. I think if you keep something bland in your stomach it settles it."

Nic's irritation was growing by the second. Brooke was a terrible liar because she believed in being honest. So much so it had gotten her into trouble a number of times. Her behavior while answering his questions demonstrated that while she hadn't actually said anything false, she was keeping things from him.

"Are you pregnant?"

"We've been careful."

"That didn't answer my question." He leaned down and grabbed her chin, pinning her with his gaze. "Are you pregnant?"

"Yes." Her voice came out small and unsure.

He sat back with a muffled curse. "Why didn't you tell me?"

"That was the plan when I came to Ithaca." She pushed into a sitting position and retreated away from him as far

as the headboard would allow. "I couldn't tell you something like that over the phone, but then I showed up and
you were so unhappy to see me." She wrapped her arms
around herself and stared at her shoes. "And then you an-
nounce that you are a prince and you need to get married so
your country could have an heir and that your wife needed
to be an aristocrat or a citizen of Sherdana."

"So you were planning on leaving without ever telling
me?" Outrage gave his voice a sharp edge.

"Don't say it like that. You made a choice to come back
here and do the honorable thing. I made a decision that
would save you from regret."

"But to never see my child?"

She put her hands over the lower half of her face and
closed her eyes. After a long moment she spoke. "Don't
you think I considered that? But I knew you would have
other children, hopefully lots of them."

Her every word slashed his heart into ribbons. The
woman he loved was having his child and he'd been days
away from never knowing the truth. "Well, there's no question of you going home now."

"What? You can't make that decision for me. My job,
friends and family are in California. That's where I belong. Just like you belong here in Sherdana with your family and your future *wife*."

She was crazy if she thought he was just going to let
her vanish out of his life. "You belong with me just like I
belong with you and our child."

"Maybe if you were the ordinary scientist I first fell in
love with, but you are a prince with responsibilities that
are bigger than both of us combined. Do the right thing
and let me go. It's the only thing that makes sense."

"I refuse to accept that." Nic got to his feet and stared
down at her. Where a moment earlier she'd seemed frag-
ile and lost, her passionate determination to do what she

perceived as the honorable thing gave her the look of a Valkyrie. "Get some rest. We will talk at length later."

Nic should have gone straight to his mother to deliver the confirmation of Brooke's condition as he'd promised, but found he needed some privacy to absorb what he'd just learned. He headed to his suite in the royal wing, curious to see if it was in the condition Gabriel had said. But just as Ariana had said, there was no leak.

The rooms that had been his growing up couldn't feel any less familiar than if he'd never seen them before. The past ten years of his life, first living in Boston, then California, felt much more real to him than the first twenty-two being Sherdana's prince. But that had been the case before he'd found out Brooke was pregnant. If he put aside duty and engaged in an honest conversation with himself, he'd accept that he no longer felt connected to his birth country. Yet his failure in the Mojave Desert meant that California was no longer a welcoming destination, either.

Never had he felt so conflicted about his future path. No matter what direction he chose, he was destined to leave disappointment and regret in his wake. Staying in Sherdana and marrying a suitable bride would require him to give up the woman he loved and abandon his child. But if he chose to make a life with Brooke could he convince her that he would never regret turning his back on his country when he knew it would always haunt him? And what would he do in California without the *Griffin* to work on? Teach at a university? He frowned.

When an hour of self-reflection passed without a clear solution presenting itself, Nic left his suite and sought his mother. He found her and his father in the king's private office deep in discussion.

"Well?" the king demanded, his eyes reflecting disappointment. He was seated behind a large mahogany desk that had been a gift from the king of Spain back in the early eighteenth century. "Is Dr. Davis pregnant?"

"Yes." Nic refused to feel like a chastised teenager. "And the child is mine." This last he directed to his mother, who sat on one of the burgundy sofas in the office's sitting area.

She was in the process of pouring a cup of tea and sent a pained look to her husband. "It seems as if none of my grandchildren are going to be legitimate."

"I won't apologize for what happened," he told his parents. "And I won't shirk my responsibility to Brooke."

"What does that mean?" his father said, his deep voice charged with warning.

"I don't have all the details worked out yet."

"You're not planning to marry her."

"It would take both of us to be on board for that to happen and at this point she's determined to return to California alone."

"You must let her," his mother said. "We will make sure she and the child are well taken of, but news of this must not get out. You need to marry and produce children that can one day succeed Gabriel."

The press of duty had never felt more overwhelming. Nic wanted to struggle free of the smothering net of responsibility that his parents cast over him.

"And what about Christian?" Nic asked, his heart burning with bitterness. "Will he not be expected to do the same?"

"Of course." The king nodded. "We are calling on both of you."

And with that, Nic accepted that one decision had been made for him.

Embarrassment and remorse kept Brooke from venturing out of her room the rest of the day. She put her pajamas back on, pulled the curtains closed and huddled in bed. A maid brought her lunch, which she barely touched, and when Ariana poked her head in the room sometime in the late afternoon, Brooke pretended to be sleeping.

She couldn't hide like this forever. For one thing it wasn't her style to avoid problems, and she really wouldn't shake the despair gnawing at her until she apologized to the queen for her outburst.

Around five she roused and phoned Theresa, needing to pour her heart out to someone who was 100 percent on her side. Unfortunately, the call rolled to voice mail and Brooke hung up without leaving a message. This was her problem to solve and the sooner she faced the music, the better.

A maid came by around six and found Brooke dressed in her tribal print maxi dress and sandals. Wearing her own clothes was like wrapping herself in a little piece of home. She didn't fit into Nic's world and trying to appear as if she did had been silly. Better to face the queen's displeasure as her authentic self, a woman who knew her own mind and was determined to do what was best for her and for Nic.

"Princess Olivia sent me to ask if you felt well enough to have dinner with her in half an hour," the maid said.

"Tell her yes."

When Brooke entered Prince Gabriel and Princess Olivia's private suite thirty minutes later, she wasn't surprised to discover Olivia had heard all about the morning's events. Up until now the princess had seemed like an ally, but would that continue? Brooke regarded Olivia warily as the princess indicated a spot on the gold couch. Brooke sat down while Olivia poured a cup of something that smelled like peppermint from a silver tea set.

The princess's kindness brought tears to Brooke's eyes. "How badly have I messed everything up?"

Olivia's eyes grew thoughtful. "Your pregnancy has

created quite a stir as you can imagine, but you shouldn't feel responsible. I doubt either you or Nic planned this."

"I don't mean that. I mean how mad is the queen that I yelled at her?"

"I didn't hear anything about that." Olivia's lips twitched and her eyes glinted with merriment. "What happened?"

"It's a bit of a blur. She said something dismissive about Nic needing to forget about the rocket and I straight up lost it." Brooke cradled the teacup, hoping the warmth would penetrate her icy fingers. "I started ranting about how he worked so hard because he wanted to justify his being away from his country for so long." Brooke shook her head as her heart contracted in shame. "It's none of my business. I shouldn't have said anything."

"You were defending the man you love. I think the queen understands."

"You didn't see her face." Brooke squinted and tried to summon a memory of the queen's reaction, but all she recalled was the garden pitching around her and the descent into darkness. "I was so rude."

"You are being too hard on yourself," Olivia said. "No wonder you and Nic get along so well. You're both such honorable people."

"I don't feel very honorable at the moment. But I'd like to change that. I made arrangements for a flight leaving the day after tomorrow at nine in the morning. I could use some help getting to the airport."

"You can't really mean to leave."

"You can't possibly think it's a good idea for me to stay. The longer I'm here the more likely it will leak that I'm pregnant. Better if I disappear from Sherdana so Nic can move forward with his life."

"What makes you think he's just going to let you go? When faced with the same choice, Gabriel fought for me.

Nic is no less an Alessandro and I don't think he's any less in love."

Olivia's words provoked many questions as Brooke realized that the princess had been confronted by a similar choice of whether to marry her prince when doing so put the future line of Alessandros at risk. But as much as curiosity nipped at her, Brooke feared asking would insult the princess.

"I think Gabriel is more of a romantic than Nic," Brooke said. "Your husband's heart led him to choose you and he will never question whether he made the right decision. Nic approaches matters with logic, listing the pros and cons, assigning values so he can rank what's most important. I think he takes after his mother in that respect."

Olivia's beautiful blue eyes clouded. "You know him well so I will just have to accept that you're right, but I hope for your sake that you're wrong."

Eleven

Both Olivia and Ariana had ganged up on Brooke and convinced her to go to the prime minister's birthday party the next evening. As it was her last night in Sherdana—she was due to fly out the next morning—the princesses were opposed to her spending any more time alone. Their concern was a balm to Brooke's battered spirit and because Ariana had tapped into her contacts in the fashion world and found Brooke the perfect Jean-Louis Scherrer gown to wear, she'd caved with barely a whimper.

Trailing into the party behind the crown prince and princess with Ariana beside her for support, Brooke experienced a sense of wonder that made her glad she'd come. The gown Ariana had found for her had the empire waist Brooke loved and a free flowing skirt. With every stride, the skirt's bright gold lining flashed and showed off the most perfect pair of Manolo Blahnik shoes with tasseled straps. The bodice was crusted with bronze beading that made her think of Moroccan embellishment and the gown's material was a subdued orange, gold and pink paisley pattern that exhibited Brooke's bohemian style.

After meeting the prime minister and wishing him a happy birthday, Brooke relaxed enough to gaze around at the guests. With Ariana at her side, no one seemed overly interested in her. It wasn't that she was ignored. Each person she was introduced to was polite and cordial, but no one seemed overly curious about the stranger from California. Brooke suspected that Ariana's social nature brought all sorts of individuals into her sphere.

Of Nic she saw nothing. The party was crowded with Sherdanian dignitaries and Brooke was determined not to spend the entire evening wondering which of the women Nic might choose to become his wife.

"Do you see what I mean about dull?" Ariana murmured to her an hour into the party. "We've made an appearance. Anytime you're ready to leave, just say the word. A friend of mine owns a club. It's opening night and he'd love to have me show up."

Brooke had been finding the party anything but dull. Unlike Nic, she liked to balance hours of study and research with socializing. People-watching was the best way to get out of her head and the prime minister's party was populated by characters.

"Sure, we can leave, but this isn't as dull as you say."

"I'm sorry, I forget that you are new to all this."

"I suppose you're right. Who is the woman in the black gown and the one over there in blue?" Each of them negotiated the room on the arm of an older gentleman, but Brooke had observed several telling glances passing between them.

"That's Countess Venuto." Ariana indicated the woman wearing blue. "And Renanta Arazzi. Her husband is the minister of trade. The men hate each other."

"Their wives don't share their husbands' antagonism."

"What do you mean?"

"I think they're having an affair." Brooke grinned. "Or they're just about to."

Ariana gasped, obviously shocked. "Tell me how you know."

Brooke spent the next hour explaining her reasoning to Ariana and then commented on several other things she'd picked up, astonishing the princess with her observations and guesses.

"You have an uncanny knack for reading people," Ariana exclaimed. "Gabriel should hire you to sit in on his meetings and advise him on people's motives."

Flattered, Brooke laughed. "I'm trained as an analyst. Whether it's art, literature or people, I guess I just dig until I locate meaning. Just don't ask me about anything having to do with numbers or technology. That's where I fail miserably."

"But that's what makes you and my brother such a perfect pairing. You complement each other."

At the mention of Nic, Brooke's good mood fled. "If only he wasn't a prince and I wasn't an ordinary girl from California." She kept her voice light, but in her chest, her heart thumped dully. "I didn't tell you earlier, but I made arrangements to fly home tomorrow morning."

"You can't leave." Ariana looked distressed. "At least stay through the wedding."

The thought of delaying the inevitable for another week made Brooke shudder. Plus, she hadn't yet been offered the opportunity to apologize to the queen in person and didn't feel right taking advantage of the king and queen's hospitality with that hanging over her. "I can't stay. Coming here in the first place was a mistake."

"But then I'd never have met you and that would have been a tragedy."

Brooke appreciated Ariana's attempt to make her feel

special. "I feel the same way about you. I just wish I'd handled things better." By which she meant the incident with the queen and Nic's discovering that she was pregnant.

She hadn't spoken to him since he'd left her room the day before. She'd dined that night with Olivia and taken both breakfast and lunch in her room. Ariana had joined her for the midday meal, bringing with her the gown Brooke was wearing tonight and reminding her of the promise she'd made to attend the birthday party.

Suddenly the crowd parted and Nic appeared, looking imposing and very princely as he strode through the room. Brooke stared at him in hopeless adoration, still unaccustomed to the effortless aura of power he assumed in his native environment. What was so different about him? He'd always radiated strength and confidence, but he'd been approachable despite his often inherent aloofness. What made him seem so inaccessible now? Was it the arrogant tilt of his head? The way he wore the expensive, custom tuxedo as easily as a T-shirt and jeans? The cool disdain in his burnished gold eyes?

And then he caught sight of her and the possessive glow of his gaze melted the chill from his features. Brooke's heart exploded in her chest and she abandoned Ariana with a quick apology, slipping through the party guests in Nic's direction before she considered what she would say. When she'd drawn to within five feet of him, her path was blocked by a petite brunette in a shimmering black mini.

"Nicolas Alessandro, I heard you returned home." The woman's cultured voice stopped Brooke dead in her tracks.

She turned aside and spotted French doors leading onto a terrace. Moving in that direction with as much haste as she dared, Brooke chastised herself. What had she been thinking? She and Nic couldn't act as friends or even acquaintances at this public event. All eyes were on the returning prince. During her self-imposed incarceration, she'd pored over the local gossip blogs and read several news articles speculating on Nic's abrupt return. The media were having a field day detailing all the women who'd been invited to the royal wedding the following week and speculating on who might be the front-runner to become the next Sherdanian princess.

Not one of the news sources had mentioned a girl from California. For that Brooke was grateful, but if she threw herself at Nic during this party, how long would it be before someone started wondering who she was.

Brooke had about five minutes of solitude on the terrace before she was joined by Olivia.

"Are you all right?" the princess inquired, her concern bringing tears to Brooke's eyes.

"I almost made a huge mistake out there. I saw Nic and raced through the crowd to get to him." Her story came out in uneven bursts as her heart continued to pound erratically. "If someone hadn't beaten me to him, I don't know what I would have done." Brooke braced herself on the metal railing as hysterical laughter bubbled up, making her knees wobble. "I am such an idiot."

"Not at all. You are in love. It makes us behave in strange and mysterious ways."

Brooke loved Olivia's British accent. It made even the most impossible statements sound plausible. Already calm was settling back over her.

"I'm so glad I had the chance to get to know you," Brooke said. "Ariana, too. Nic is lucky to have you."

"He'd be lucky to have you as well if only you wouldn't be so eager to rush off."

"I know you mean well." Brooke shook her head. "But Nic needs me to go."

"What if instead he really needs you to stay? He's been locked in the library since yesterday morning. His mind is a hundred miles away from anyone trying to have a conversation with him. He called Christian and could be heard yelling at him to get home all the way across the palace."

That didn't sound much like the Nic she knew, but then he'd been through a lot in the past month. Was it any surprise that having his entire world turned upside down would cause a crack in his relentless confidence?

"It's my fault," Brooke said, her own confidence returning. "I dropped a huge bomb on him yesterday when I said I was going back to California without consulting him."

"You should speak to him. He wants badly to do right by everyone and it's tearing him apart."

As it had torn Brooke apart, until she'd concluded that Nic would be better off not knowing about her pregnancy. "But I'm leaving in the morning. It will have to be tonight." Brooke considered. "Ariana's friend has a club opening tonight and she wants to go. I'll have her drop me at the palace. If you'll let Nic know, I'll be waiting for him in the library at midnight."

She didn't want him to leave the party early. His mother would expect him to spend the evening getting acquainted with all the available women there. Brooke turned to go, but Olivia stopped her.

"If Nic could marry you, would you accept?"

The princess asked the question with such poignant sincerity that Brooke faced her and answered in kind. "I love him with everything I am. Which is why it's both incredibly simple and impossibly hard to let him go so he can be the prince his family needs him to be."

Olivia wrapped her in a fierce hug and whispered, "If he asks you to stay, please say yes."

Brooke smiled at the beautiful princess without answering and then squared her shoulders and went to find Ariana.

* * *

Trapped in a tedious conversation with one of Christian's former girlfriends, Alexia Le Mans, Nic watched Brooke exit the ballroom for the less populated terrace and was just extricating himself to go after her when Olivia beat him to it. He'd only come to the party tonight in the hopes of seeing Brooke and demanding they have a conversation about the child she carried. He might not be able to marry her, but he'd be damned if the child would disappear out of his life. Nic had seen Gabriel's regret at not knowing his daughters during their first two years and Nic wasn't going to let that happen to him.

Ten minutes after Brooke left the room, she was back, and almost immediately he lost her in the crush. He moved to intercept her, but was stopped three times before he reached where he thought Brooke had been headed.

"Nic."

He turned at Olivia's voice and saw that she and Gabriel were coming up behind him. "I can't talk right now, I'm looking for Brooke."

Olivia exchanged a wordless look with her husband. "Ariana was heading to a club opening and she offered to give Brooke a lift back to the palace. But before she left, she gave me a message for you. She said she'll be waiting to speak to you in the library at midnight."

"Thank you." Nic had no intention of waiting until then to talk with Brooke. "And thank you for all you've done for her."

"No need to thank me," Olivia said, her smile affectionate. "She's lovely and I've enjoyed being her friend."

"Yes," Gabriel added. "Too bad she couldn't become a permanent fixture in the palace. I think she'd make an outstanding princess."

The temptation to say something disrespectful to the future king sizzled in Nic's mind, but he quelled his frustration and thanked Olivia with as much courtesy as he could muster. Bidding them goodbye, Nic headed downstairs to reclaim his car and follow Brooke to the palace.

The drive from the hotel where the prime minister's party had taken place back to the palace only took ten minutes, but Nic discovered Brooke had already disappeared into the visitors' wing by the time he arrived. He'd hoped to catch her before she went upstairs so they could have their conversation someplace that wouldn't invite gossip, but that wasn't going to stop him from tracking her down.

As he knocked on her door, he was a little out of breath from his rush up the stairs to the third floor. Listening to his heart thunder in his chest as he waited for her to answer, he made a note to drink less and exercise more than had been his habit in the past month. But when Brooke answered the door, snatching his breath away as he stared down into her soft gray-green eyes, he knew it wasn't stamina that had caused his heart and lungs to labor, but excitement at being close to her again.

"Nic? What are you doing here?"

"You wanted to talk." He stepped forward, forcing her to retreat into her room. As soon as he cleared the door, he shut it behind him. His hands made short work of his tie and slipped the first buttons of his shirt free. "Let's talk."

Brooke's body immediately began to thrum with arousal at Nic's apparent intent in entering her room. Her lips couldn't form protests as he removed his tuxedo jacket and unfastened his gold cuff links. Those went into his pocket before he set the jacket on a convenient chair while still advancing on her.

"Didn't Olivia tell you midnight in the library?"

"I considered it a suggested time and place." He pulled his shirt free of his pants and went back to work on the b tons. Each one he freed gave her a more evocative glimpse of the impressive chest beneath. "I prefer this one."

The gold shards in Nic's eyes brightened perceivably when his temper was aroused. Because she enjoyed riling him, Brooke had noticed this phenomenon a lot. She could judge the level of his agitation by the degree of the sparkle. At the moment his gaze was almost too intense to meet.

She thought about Olivia's words and wished he'd ask her to stay in Sherdana. No, she didn't. She ached for him to ask her. But he wouldn't. He shouldn't. From the start he'd been right to keep her at bay.

Nic closed the distance between them and swept her into his arms. As he bent her backward, his lips gliding along her temple, Brooke's senses spun.

"Stay in Sherdana a while longer."

He wasn't asking for forever, but every second with him was precious. "I don't belong here."

"Neither do I," he whispered an instant before his lips met hers.

With a moan, she sank her fingers into his thick black hair and held on as he fed off her mouth. Desire lashed at her, setting her pent-up emotions free. She met him kiss for kiss, claiming him as he sought to brand her with his passion.

Both were breathing unevenly when he lifted his lips from hers and captured her gaze. With her heart thundering in her ears, Brooke barely heard his words.

"You and I belong together."

"In another life. As different people. I'd give up everything to be with you," she murmured, the last of her resistance crumbling as he slid his hands down her back and aligned her curves to his granite muscles. "But not here and now."

"Yes to here and now," he growled. "It's tomorrow and

all the days beyond we can't have. Don't deny either of us this last night of happiness."

Brooke surrendered to the flood of longing and the demanding pressure of his arms banded around her body. Tomorrow would come all too soon. She wanted him for as long as possible.

With her face pressed against his bare chest, her ear tuned to the steady beat of his heart, she said, "I love you."

His arms crushed her, preventing any further words. For a long moment his grip stopped her from breathing, and then his hold gentled.

"You are the only woman I'll ever love."

Brooke lifted up on tiptoe and pushed her lips against his. He immediately opened to her and she matched the fierce hunger of his kiss with a desperation she couldn't hide. He loved her.

Working with deliberation that made her ache, he eased down the zipper of her dress, his lips sending a line of fire along her skin as he went. She'd never felt so adored as he unwrapped her body, treating her as if she was a precious gift. By the time his fingers lifted away the exquisite designer gown, exposing all of her, she was quivering uncontrollably.

Nic stripped away the last of her clothes, pushed her to arm's length and stared. Looking at her excited him and that set her blood on fire. She licked her dry lips and his pupils flared, almost vanquishing his gold irises. Her legs trembled. She couldn't take much more without ending up in a heap at his feet.

Without warning he surged back to life, lifting her into his arms and carrying her to the bed. As she floated down to land on the mattress, Brooke's thighs parted in welcome and Nic quickly stripped off the rest of his clothes and covered her with his body. She expected him to surge inside her, such was the intensity of his erection, but instead, he went back to work on her body with lips and hands, driving her to impossible levels of hunger.

At long last, she'd gone light-years past the point of readiness and gathered handfuls of his hair. "I can't wait any longer to have you inside me."

"Are you asking or commanding?" He sucked hard on her neck and she quaked.

"I'm begging." She reached down and found him. Her firm grip wrenched a satisfying moan from his lips. "Please, Nic."

His hands spanned her hips and in one swift thrust he answered her plea. She flexed her spine and accepted his full length while he devoured her impassioned groan. Before she could grow accustomed to the feel of him filling her, Nic rolled them over until she sat astride his hips.

This new position offered a different set of sensations and freed his hands to cruise across her torso at will. She took charge of their lovemaking and began to move. Whispering words of encouragement, he cupped her breasts, kneading and rolling her hard nipples between his fingers to intensify her pleasure.

When she came, it was hard and fast. If she could have lingered in the moment forever, she would have known perfect happiness, but such profound ecstasy wasn't meant to last. And there was a different sort of joy in the lazy aftermath of being so thoroughly loved. As Nic nuzzled his face in the place where her neck met her shoulder, Brooke savored the synchronized beat of their hearts and knew no matter where her body existed, her soul would stay with Nic where it belonged.

Morning brought rain and the distant rumble of thunder. Nic woke to the soft, fragrant sweetness of Brooke's naked body curved against his and held his breath to keep from disturbing the magic of the moment. Last night had been incredible. And it had been goodbye. He'd tasted it in the desperation of her kisses and felt it in the wildness of his need for her.

"What time is it?" she asked, her voice a contented purr.

"A little before seven."

"Oh." She practically sprang out of bed and began to hunt around for her clothes. "I have to go."

Nic sat up, automatically admiring the fluid movement of her nude form as she dressed. "Where are you going?"

"Home. My flight leaves in two hours."

Shock held him motionless and she'd almost reached the door before he caught up with her. If he hadn't barged into her room and spent the night would he have even known she was gone?

"And if I ask you to stay?" He thought he was ready to set her free, but now that the moment had arrived, he was incapable of saying goodbye.

"Don't you mean command?" Her smile was both wicked and sad.

Despite his solemn mood, Nic's lips twitched. "You aren't Sherdanian. I have no way to make you behave."

"And throwing me in the dungeon would create an international scandal that would upset your mother."

"Is that why you're running away? Because you think either I or my family would be bothered by some adverse publicity?"

Her body stiffened. "I'm not running away. I'm returning to California where I live. Just like you are staying in Sherdana where you belong. Besides, the longer I stay the more I risk becoming fodder for the tabloids and that wouldn't do your marriage hunt any favors."

"No. I suppose it wouldn't. But I still don't want you to go."

"And yet I must."

"You're breaking my heart," he said, carrying her hand to his lips and placing her palm against his bare chest.

"I'm breaking *your* heart?" She tugged her hand from beneath his, but his free arm snaked around her, and pulled her resistant body against him. "Do you have any idea how unfair you're being right now?"

He knew and didn't care. Nic tightened his hold, letting his heat seep into her until there was no more resistance. And then he kissed her, long and slow and deep, while in the back of his mind he acknowledged that this would be their final goodbye. By the time he broke away they were both gasping for breath.

Brooke spoke first. "You were right."

"About?" He nuzzled her cheek, feathering provocative kisses along her skin. His teeth grazed her earlobe, making her shudder.

"Starting something that had no future." Her pain and grief tore at him.

"I didn't want there to be regrets between us."

"I don't regret it."

"But you can't help thinking if we'd never been together that leaving would be easier." His arms tightened. "And you might be right. But for the rest of my life I will cherish every second we've spent together." And now he had to be strong enough to let her go. Only knowing that their child would connect them together forever gave him the courage to set her free. "There's no getting you out of my system," he said. "Or my heart."

"I love you." She kissed him one last time. "Now let me go."

Twelve

"You let her go?" Gabriel Alessandro, crown prince of Sherdana, was furious. "What the hell is the matter with you?"

From her seat behind the ornate writing desk, Olivia watched her husband storm around the living room of their suite, her expression a mask of sadness and resignation.

"Why are you yelling at me?" Nic demanded, pointing at Gabriel's princess. "She's the one who arranged to have a car take her to the airport."

It was shortly before lunch and Brooke's flight had departed Carone International over two hours prior. By now she would be over the Atlantic Ocean on her way to New York's JFK airport and her connecting flight to San Francisco.

"It's not my wife's fault that she was leaving in the first place. You were supposed to stop her before she ever got into the car." Gabriel raked his fingers through his hair in a gesture of acute frustration. "Do you realize what you've done?"

"I did what the country required of me."

Silence greeted his declaration, but Nic refused to feel bad that he'd at long last addressed the elephant in the room. He'd let Brooke get away because Gabriel hadn't acted in the country's best interest when he'd married Olivia.

"For the first time in your life," Gabriel shouted back. "How the hell do you think I felt having to carry the burden of responsibility for both you and Christian all these years? Maybe I would have enjoyed being an irresponsible playboy or playing at an impossible dream like building a rocket ship."

"Playing at—"

"Enough." Olivia's sharp tone sliced through the testosterone thickening the air and silenced both men. "Tossing accusations back and forth is not solving our immediate issue."

Gabriel was the first to back down. He turned to his wife and the love that glowed in his gaze made Nic's heart hurt.

"She's right." Gabriel's attention returned to his brother. "I know you were doing amazing things in California and I wish you were still there doing them. I really don't begrudge you any time you've spent chasing your dream."

Nic was seeing a different side of his brother. Never before had Gabriel spoken so eloquently about what he was feeling. The crown prince could speak passionately about issues relating to the country and he had a fine reputation for diplomacy, but he'd always been a closed book with regard to anything of a personal nature.

"I've lost my nerve." Since Gabriel felt comfortable sharing, Nic decided it was only fair to give a little in return. "Since the accident, I am afraid to even think about what went wrong with *Griffin*. Five years of my life went into designing the fuel delivery system that caused the rocket to blow up. I killed someone. There's no coming back from that for me." Nic's voice was thick with regret as he finished, "It's part of the reason I let Brooke go. Her life is in California and there's no place for me there anymore. I belong here where I can make a difference."

"Oh, Nic." Olivia was at his side, her soft hand gentle on his arm. "I'm sorry you are in so much pain. And what happened to your rocket and that man's death are a horrible tragedy, but you can't let that get in the way of your happiness with Brooke."

Gabriel grabbed his other arm and gave him a shake. "And you really don't belong here."

"Yes, I do. The country needs an heir to the throne." But his protest was cut short as Olivia and Gabriel shared a moment of intense nonverbal communication. "What's going on?"

Olivia shifted her gaze to Nic and offered him a sympathetic head tilt. "We can't get into specifics…"

"About what?" There was obviously an important secret being kept from him and Nic didn't like being left out.

The crown prince's lips quirked in a wry smile. "What if as the future leader of your country I order you to return to California, resume work on your rocket ship and marry the mother of your child?"

Nic spent a long moment grappling with his conscience. He'd come to grips with sacrificing his happiness for the sake of the country and although it had torn him apart to let Brooke go, he'd known it was for the greater good of Sherdana and his family.

Now, however, his brother was offering him a way out. No, Nic amended. Gabriel was directing him to forsake his duty and chase his dreams all the way back to California. The walls he'd erected to garrison his misery began to crumble. He sucked in a ragged breath. Permission to marry Brooke and raise their child with her. The chance to complete his dream of space travel. All on a silver platter compliments of his brother. It was too much.

But as he scrutinized Gabriel's confident posture and observed the secret smile that lit Olivia's eyes, he sensed that whatever was going on, these two were well in control of the country's future.

Nic offered Gabriel a low bow, his throat tight. "Naturally, I'd do whatever my crowned prince commands."

On her way to the Mojave Air and Space Port to visit her brother, Brooke took a familiar detour and drove past the house Nic had rented for the past three years. The place looked as deserted as ever. Nic hadn't spent much time there, sometimes not even sleeping in his own bed for days at a stretch because the couch in his workroom was within arm's reach of his project.

Still, when she could get him to take time off, they'd often had fun barbecuing in the backyard or drinking beer on the front porch while they stared at the stars and Nic opened up about what he and Glen hoped one day to accomplish.

Brooke stomped on the accelerator and her Prius picked up speed. Those days were behind her now that Nic was back in Sherdana, but at least she had the memories.

A ten-minute drive through town brought her to the hangar where Glen and his team were working on the new rocket. Brooke hadn't been here since the day Nic had broken off with her and she was surprised how little work had been done. From what Glen had told her, the inflow of cash hadn't dried up after the first *Griffin* had exploded. In fact, the mishap had alerted several new investors who'd promised funding for the project.

Brooke spent several minutes walking around the platform that held the skeleton of the *Griffin II*, her footsteps echoing around the empty hangar. She wasn't accustomed to this level of inactivity and wondered if she'd misunderstood her brother's text, asking her to meet him at the airfield rather than at his house.

As she made her way to the back of the facility where the workrooms and labs were set up, Brooke detected faint strains of music and figured her brother had gotten caught up in something and lost track of time. Except the music wasn't coming from Glen's office, but from Nic's former workroom.

The wave of sorrow that swarmed over her stopped Brooke in her tracks. Someone had obviously been hired to replace Nic on the team and had been given his office. The shock of it made her dizzy, but she quickly rationalized the unsteadiness away. How could she expect forward progress on the rocket without someone taking on the fuel delivery system Nic had abandoned? With the exception of her brother, no one else on the team could match Nic's brilliance or comprehend the intricacies of his design. Someone new would have to be brought in.

Brooke squared her shoulders and continued down the hallway. She might as well introduce herself to Nic's replacement and start to accept the changes that he'd bring to the team.

"Hi," she called over the music as she first knocked, and then pushed open the unlatched door. "I'm Brooke Davis, Glen's..." Her voice trailed away as the tall man in jeans and a black T-shirt turned to greet her.

"Sister," Nic finished for her. "He told me you might be stopping by today."

Brooke's throat tightened. "What are you doing here?"

"I work here." His smile—at once familiar and utterly different from anything she'd seen before—knocked the breath from her lungs.

"I don't understand." She sagged back against the door frame and drank in Nic's presence. His vibrant, imposing presence made it impossible for her to believe he was a hallucination, but she couldn't let herself trust this amazing turn of fortune until she knew what was going on. "I left you in Sherdana. You were going to get married and make Alessandro heirs."

Nic shook his head. "Turns out I was completely wrong for the job."

"How so?" His wry amusement was beginning to reach through her shock. She was starting to thaw out. The ice water that had filled her veins for the past week heated beneath his sizzling regard. "You're not impotent or something, are you?"

He laughed and reached out to snag her wrist, pulling her away from the wall and up against his hard body. "That was not the problem."

"Then what was?" She wrapped her arms around his neck and arched her back until they were aligned from chest to thigh.

"No one wanted me."

"I can't believe that." And she didn't. Not for a single second.

"It's true. Word got around that a spunky redhead had stolen my heart and left me but a shell of a man."

Brooke purred as he bent his head and nuzzled his lips into her neck. "So you've come here to take it back?"

"No. I've come here to sign it over all legal and such."

Fearing she'd misunderstood what he was saying, Brooke remained silent while her mind worked furiously. He'd left Sherdana and resumed his old position on the team. From the way his lips were exploring her neck, she was pretty sure he intended that their physical relationship would get back on track.

"Brooke?" He cupped her face and stared deep into her eyes. "You're awfully quiet."

"I guess I'm not sure what to say."

"You could start by saying yes."

Relief made her giddy. "You haven't asked me a question."

"You're right." And to her absolute delight, he dropped down on one knee and fished a ring out of his pocket. "Brooke Davis, love of my life and mother of my child, will you marry me?"

She set her hands on her hips and shook her head. "If this is about the baby, I assure you I'm not expecting you—"

"Oh, for heaven sakes," came an explosive shout from the hallway behind them. "Just tell the guy yes."

"Yes," she whispered, leaning down to plant her lips on Nic's.

He wrapped his arms around her and shot to his feet, lifting her into the air and spinning her in circles. She laughed, delirious with joy, and hugged him back. When he let her toes touch the floor once more, Glen was there to pound Nic on the back and offer his congratulations.

Amidst this, Nic slipped an enormous diamond ring onto her left hand. She ogled it while Glen played the brother card and threatened Nic with bodily harm if he didn't take good care of her. Then Glen left her and Nic alone so he could fill her in on what had transpired after she'd left.

"Gabriel almost killed me when he heard that you'd left," Nic explained, sitting on his couch and pulling her onto his lap.

She let her head fall onto his shoulder and savored the contentment that wove through her. "He did?"

"Apparently he decided to play matchmaker and wasn't particularly happy that I failed to do my part."

"Matchmaker?"

"He made sure we were in adjoining rooms in the visitors' wing of the palace and enlisted Olivia and Ariana to convince you not to give up on us."

"They did a pretty good job of that," Brooke agreed, thinking about that last night she'd spent with Nic. "In fact, I almost left without seeing you one final time, but both of them convinced me I owed it to us to say goodbye." But there was something she still didn't understand. "And we did. I left and you didn't stop me. You were determined to do the honorable thing and stay in Sherdana and get married. So what's changed?"

"Two things. First, I thought long and hard about what made me happy. Spending the rest of my life with you and my work. But I couldn't marry you without regretting that I'd decided not to step up when my family needed me and I couldn't see returning to the *Griffin* project when my design had caused a man's death."

"And yet you're here," Brooke pointed out.

"I didn't accept I couldn't live without you until I had to start."

"But what about Sherdana and producing an heir?"

"Gabriel released me from duty. Before I left he explained how it had nearly destroyed him to lose Olivia and he refused to let me go through the same sort of pain."

"But what about an heir for the throne?"

"I guess it's up to Christian."

"And you don't feel bad that he has to carry the full burden of the country's future on his shoulders?" Brooke arched her eyebrow at Nic's poor attempt to conceal a grin.

"If he had to choose between the woman of his dreams and duty to Sherdana, I'd feel horrible." Nic brushed Brooke's hair aside and kissed his way down her neck. "But he's never dated any woman long enough to fall in love and it's time he let someone in."

"Et benedetto il primo dolce affanno ch'i' ebbi ad esser con Amor congiunto."

Nic translated, "And blessed be the first sweet agony I suffered when I found myself bound to Love." He grazed his lips against Brooke's, making her sigh in pleasure. "I only hope the woman who finally breaks through to Christian makes him half as happy as you've made me."

Heart singing, Brooke wrapped her arms around Nic's neck and set her forehead against his. His gaze fastened on hers, letting her glimpse his joy and his need for her. For the first time she truly understood the depth of Nic's love for her. He'd made light of his decision to leave Sherdana, but she suspected even though Gabriel had released him from duty, the king and queen hadn't backed either of their sons' actions.

"I haven't begun to make you happy," she promised, tightening her hold.

"You don't say."

"I do say." And she proceeded to demonstrate how she planned to start.

* * * * *

If you loved this SHERDANA ROYALS *novel,*
read more in this series from
author favorite Cat Schield

ROYAL HEIRS REQUIRED

Or pick up Cat's LAS VEGAS NIGHTS *series*

AT ODDS WITH THE HEIRESS
A MERGER BY MARRIAGE
A TASTE OF TEMPTATION

Available now from Harlequin Desire!

If you're on Twitter, tell us what you think of
Harlequin Desire! #harlequindesire

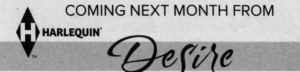
#2395 Claimed
The Diamond Tycoons • by Tracy Wolff
Diamond tycoon Marc has never forgiven his ex-fiancée for the betrayal that nearly destroyed his empire. So when a new threat links to Isabella, he vows to keep his enemy by his side—and in his bed—until he uncovers the truth...

#2396 The Baby Contract
Billionaires and Babies • by Barbara Dunlop
Security expert Tony won't hire Mila as a security specialist—but he will hire her to care for the baby that has come under his protection. Working together night and day soon turns this job into a passionate mission...

#2397 Maid for a Magnate
Dynasties: The Montoros • by Jules Bennett
Businessman Will Rowling fell for Catalina Iberra when they were young, but dating his father's maid was a no-no. Will one random kiss—and getting stranded on a deserted island!—take them back to where they left off?

#2398 His Son, Her Secret
The Beaumont Heirs • by Sarah M. Anderson
When Byron Beaumont returns to Colorado after a year away, he's stunned to find that his ex—the daughter of his family's nemesis—secretly had Byron's son. Now he's determined to claim them both—whatever it takes!

#2399 Bidding on Her Boss
The Hawke Brothers • by Rachel Bailey
When a florist buys her boss at auction, not for a date but to pitch a business idea, he's impressed...and unexpectedly finds himself falling for the last person he should get involved with—his own employee!

#2400 Only on His Terms
The Accidental Heirs • by Elizabeth Bevarly
It turns out Gracie Summer's kind, elderly neighbor wasn't a retired repairman, but a reclusive billionaire who left her all his money! It'll be tough convincing his dangerously attractive son that she's innocent of any scheming...especially if they fall for each other.

REQUEST YOUR FREE BOOKS!
2 FREE NOVELS PLUS 2 FREE GIFTS!

HARLEQUIN®

Desire

ALWAYS POWERFUL, PASSIONATE AND PROVOCATIVE

YES! Please send me 2 FREE Harlequin® Desire novels and my 2 FREE gifts (gifts are worth about $10). After receiving them, if I don't wish to receive any more books, I can return the shipping statement marked "cancel." If I don't cancel, I will receive 6 brand-new novels every month and be billed just $4.55 per book in the U.S. or $5.24 per book in Canada. That's a savings of at least 13% off the cover price! It's quite a bargain! Shipping and handling is just 50¢ per book in the U.S. and 75¢ per book in Canada.* I understand that accepting the 2 free books and gifts places me under no obligation to buy anything. I can always return a shipment and cancel at any time. Even if I never buy another book, the two free books and gifts are mine to keep forever.

225/326 HDN GH2P

Name	(PLEASE PRINT)	
Address		Apt. #
City	State/Prov.	Zip/Postal Code

Signature (if under 18, a parent or guardian must sign)

Mail to the **Reader Service:**
IN U.S.A.: P.O. Box 1867, Buffalo, NY 14240-1867
IN CANADA: P.O. Box 609, Fort Erie, Ontario L2A 5X3

Want to try two free books from another line?
Call 1-800-873-8635 or visit www.ReaderService.com.

* Terms and prices subject to change without notice. Prices do not include applicable taxes. Sales tax applicable in N.Y. Canadian residents will be charged applicable taxes. Offer not valid in Quebec. This offer is limited to one order per household. Not valid for current subscribers to Harlequin Desire books. All orders subject to credit approval. Credit or debit balances in a customer's account(s) may be offset by any other outstanding balance owed by or to the customer. Please allow 4 to 6 weeks for delivery. Offer available while quantities last.

Your Privacy—The Reader Service is committed to protecting your privacy. Our Privacy Policy is available online at www.ReaderService.com or upon request from the Reader Service.

We make a portion of our mailing list available to reputable third parties that offer products we believe may interest you. If you prefer that we not exchange your name with third parties, or if you wish to clarify or modify your communication preferences, please visit us at www.ReaderService.com/consumerschoice or write to us at Reader Service Preference Service, P.O. Box 9062, Buffalo, NY 14240-9062. Include your complete name and address.

HDI5

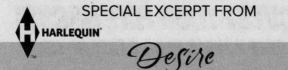
Isabella was somehow even more beautiful than he'd remembered. And probably more treacherous, Marc reminded himself as he fought for control.

It had been six years since he'd seen her.

Six years since he'd held her, kissed her, made love to her.

Six years since he'd kicked her out of his apartment and his life.

And still, he wanted her.

It came as something of a shock, considering he'd done his best not to think about her in the ensuing years.

All it had taken was a glimpse of her gorgeous red hair, her warm brown eyes, from the small window embedded in the classroom door to throw him right back into the seething, tumultuous heat that had characterized so much of their relationship. He hadn't cared about anything but getting into that room to see if his mind was playing tricks on him.

Six years ago he had kicked Isa Varin—now, apparently, Isabella Moreno—out of his life in the cruelest manner possible. He didn't regret making her leave—how could he when she'd betrayed him so completely?—but in the time since, he had regretted how he'd done it. When he'd come to his senses and sent his driver to find her and deliver her things, including her purse and cell phone and some money, she had vanished into thin air. He'd looked for her, but he'd never found her.

Now he knew why. The very passionate, very beautiful, very bewitching Isa Varin had ceased to exist. In her place was this buttoned-down professor, her voice and face as cool and sharp as any diamond his mines had ever produced. Only the hair—that glorious red hair—was the same. Isabella Moreno wore it in a tight braid down her back instead of in the wild curls favored by his Isa, but he would know the color anywhere.

Black cherries at midnight.

Wet garnets shining in the filtered light of a full moon.

And when her eyes had met his over the heads of her students, he'd felt a punch in his gut—in his groin—that couldn't be denied. Only Isa had ever made his body react so powerfully.

One look into her eyes used to bring him to his knees. But those days were long gone. Her betrayal had destroyed any faith he might have had in her. He'd been weak once, had fallen for the innocence she could project with a look, a touch, a whisper.

He wouldn't make that mistake again.

Will Marc have Isa back in his bed, trust be damned?

Find out in CLAIMED, the first of the DIAMOND TYCOONS duet by New York Times bestselling author Tracy Wolff, available wherever Harlequin® Desire books and ebooks are sold.

www.Harlequin.com

HARLEQUIN®

A *Romance* FOR EVERY MOOD™

JUST CAN'T GET ENOUGH?

Join our social communities
and talk to us online.

You will have access to the latest
news on upcoming titles and special
promotions, but most importantly,
you can talk to other fans about your
favorite Harlequin reads.

Harlequin.com/Community

 Facebook.com/HarlequinBooks

 Twitter.com/HarlequinBooks

 Pinterest.com/HarlequinBooks

THE WORLD IS BETTER WITH

Romance

Harlequin has everything from contemporary, passionate and heartwarming to suspenseful and inspirational stories.

Whatever your mood, we have a romance just for you!

Connect with us to find your next great read, special offers and more.

f /HarlequinBooks

🐦 @HarlequinBooks

www.HarlequinBlog.com

www.Harlequin.com/Newsletters